RO ___ ___

OF THE WILD

Also by H. Mortimer Batten
The Golden Book of Animal Stories
Tales of Wild Bird Life

ROMANCES
OF THE WILD

H. Mortimer Batten

Illustrated by Warwick Reynolds

BLACKIE: GLASGOW AND LONDON

First published 1922
Second edition 1948
Third edition 1959
Reprinted 1960, 1964, 1966
Fourth edition 1976

ISBN   o   216   90278   9 (hardback)
ISBN   o   216   90279   7 (paperback)

Blackie and Son Limited
Bishopbriggs, Glasgow G64 2NZ
450/452 Edgware Road, London W2 1EG

Printed in Great Britain by Robert MacLehose & Co. Ltd
Printers to the University of Glasgow

CONTENTS

ROMANCES
OF THE WILD

NEGEET OF THE BLUE
UNDERWORLD

I

The winter was phenomenal that year in the length and vigour of its cold snap, which came early and was succeeded by months of mild, wet weather. While the Frost King reigned the river sank below its summer level, its minor tributaries frozen to their very beds, while each pool between the rapid stretches was ice-bound, save for a channel down its centre, where the foam flakes moved with a glassy sluggishness significant of extreme cold. Even for Negeet, the otter, who of all the wild folk was best able to supply her mortal needs, it was a time of hunger, for the trout, torpid with cold, hid among the rocks at the river bed, and only for an hour or so when the sun was at its zenith did they sally forth in search of food.

Thus Negeet was forced to angle in the full light of day, and often little groups of spectators on the high-road at the mountain foot watched her as she dived back and forth from the ice, appearing at intervals in the central channel with a trout between her jaws. And thus, betrayed to all, Negeet became the common sport of many.

In the river the otter was safe. She could have lived for days beneath the ice had occasion demanded, for the sinking of the water-level since the first relentless frost had resulted in an air space surrounding every rock. It was at night-time that deadly peril beset her steps, for her hunger led her far afield, and everywhere the snow betrayed her. It is surprising how a spell of hunger upsets the whole order of things in the wild, and soon it was learnt that Negeet was given to wandering through the village during the darkest hours. She had visited several rubbish-heaps and closely inspected the most opulent hen-roosts, finding the latter barred and shuttered, for which she had to thank Mr. Reynard. And so traps were set for her, and dogs left loose to guard their masters' property.

Negeet had no knowledge of traps; like all her tribe, she seemed to possess no guarding instinct against such devices, and thus one night, attracted by a delicious odour wafted seductively to the river edge, the otter slid across the frozen high-way and through the boundary-wall by way of a draining-gully. Strewn on the ground on the other side of the wall were the entrails of a chicken, but as with eager steps the hungry otter

hurried to the feast, there was a movement beneath her, a vicious thud, and she became aware
of a terrorizing pain in both her forepaws. Instantly dormant instincts awoke; she was thrilled
with the inherited terror of the trap, and with a snarl
she splintered her splendid teeth on the remorseless steel. Desperate, frenzied fear possessed her
—she rolled, she dragged, she wrenched with all
her strength, and then—O horror!—a huge black
shape, towering, yellow-eyed, appeared against
the sky on the wall-top directly above her head.

Negeet mastered her fears and " froze ", watching with deadly preparedness, while the great
shaggy sheep-dog glowered down at her with
savage inquiry. He had come in absolute silence,
which made his sudden appearance all the more
sinister, and only a second did it take him to
assure himself that here attack was justified. He
did not know Negeet, he had never seen her
before, but this he knew—that she was not of
man's threshold, and therefore a trespasser. With
a thunderous growl he fell upon her. The full
fury of his rush was checked by Negeet's imprisoned paws and the already straining jaws of
the rusty trap.

There was a faint " click ", and Negeet was
free—no, not free, for the sheep-dog had her by
the loose skin of the back in a strangling, worrying grip! She turned upon him like a thousand
furies, and her terrible jaws got to work. Quick
as a weasel was Negeet, and her bite was terrible.
The sheep-dog loosened his hold with a yell of
surprise and pain, and the otter slid, as she had

come, into the broad highway, vaguely phosphorescent under the stars.

Another sheep-dog barred her way, and yet
another, dashing noisily to the scene. They were
brave dogs, schooled to the hard life of the hills,
but the otter, flattened out, seemed to glide between them, and when she struck—as assuredly
she did—it was the strike of a whip-snake, too
swift for human eye to perceive. She slid into a
thorn bush, the dogs following tumultuously,
though somehow the idea of closing seemed to
have lost its former attractions. Negeet dropped
a sheer ten feet over the stone breastwork built
to resist the floods, slid on her stomach down the
steep bank and out across the ice, while behind
her teemed the cascade of dogs, to stand in a
shivering, whining row, watching the rings of her
departure widen across the flood.

Negeet had learnt the lesson of her life. She
had learnt steel traps, and Nimrod and all his
followers could not have outwitted her now. She
had learnt dogs; knew that their strength lay in
their unity of purpose, and that they were closely
associated with man. Most of all she had learnt
man himself, for everywhere was the scent of him
—on the trap, on the road, yes, on the very
hateful dogs! The taint was stamped indelibly
on her memory, the whole nightmare of events
was saturated with it; and encountering that
scent in later days, Negeet turned back, or stole
by shadowy and devious routes to a place of
safety.

On the high-road above there was blood, blood

everywhere, the tracks of many dogs, and here and there the tracks of an otter. In the small hours the veterinary surgeon came from the next village on his motor-cycle, cursing the cold, cursing the villagers for leaving their dogs at large, but most of all cursing the otter, the cause of the whole disturbance.

II

After this experience Negeet would doubtless have left the locality, save for one strange custom, or law—or call it what you will—of the otter kind. Old Sam Inman, the angler, in whose company one always was aware of the poetry of his calling, first told me about it; and later on, when I came to know Negeet and her children's children, when I came to dread a change in even the smallest of the riverside kindred as old Sam dreaded such things, when I learnt what the driving mists sang to him in the alder trees, and why the river was never dull, winter or summer, day or night, most of all when I came to love that quiet valley—how well, alas, I did not understand till long, long after!—I saw that what he said was true.

" She will not go," he told me, in his quiet voice. " Mawakee, her mother, is gone, but Negeet will remain with us till next autumn— if she lives."

I wondered at this, for I had always regarded the otter as a creature as restless as the silver streams it loves, and when I said so, old Sam pursued: "Yes, but not a young *she* otter. The dogs of the litter leave the locality of their birth the first autumn, probably with their parents, but the she kits remain for another year. I suppose it is some provision of nature," he said. "In the wild there is a reason for everything, and Negeet will be with us till the spates again bring the salmon—*then she will go*!" This he added in a faintly regretful voice, as though her going would mark for him another notch in the passage of time—time being the only thing that mattered in his quiet, uneventful life. An idle life, perhaps, and yet—where is the world's city where one can earn such wealth as was daily his?

The frost went at last, and there followed days and nights of drifting cloud wraiths, when the laughter of the river seemed a mockery amidst the tearful drip of the alders and the driving blast of the mist. Sometimes, when the storm lifted, Negeet would mount the bank, and gaze with head aloft at the village lights twinkling across the moistness, their glow reflected in the wonder of her eyes. She was an endlessly lovely creature; graceful in every poise she took, swift as the shadows, silent, gliding in her movements, and when she rested no man can say. With the going of the ice she lost the listlessness of hunger. All day, though few saw her, she glided and gambolled in and out of the corridors between the boulders of the river bank. At sundown she would fish for an hour or so, then she would amuse herself by swimming up the pools, drifting back, stretching herself luxuriously, while the current caught her and bore her under the whirling stars—drew her into the maw of the whirlpool, round, round, into its very vortex. All these mighty forces were at her bidding, and easily, idly she moulded them to her will. She would cast herself belly upwards and drift, drift over the glassy bank of the fall, to be whirled with the pounding surf far out across the pool; and when the silver dawn crept through the pine-wood on the east, filling the scented spray with flashing, rainbow tints, when the dipper's merry call rang from the mossy rocks, and the sandpiper came whirling by on hooped and drooping wings, she would seek her den, refreshed, happy, but never weary. And so she lived her life—boundless in those riches used more sparingly than gold in the world of men and women.

One night a strange otter appeared below the whirlpool in Colgarth Water. He was larger than Negeet, less tapered and graceful in build, while the gray of his muzzle indicated that he was older than she—probably four summers. He had come from the sea, travelling night by night, passing beneath gloomy arches on his way, where the myriad lights of mighty cities peered down at him like unblinking stars; but now man's last droning outpost was left behind, and the scent of the heather was in the air.

Negeet rose to meet him. She was shy and suspicious, hovering on the downstream side to catch his body scent, while he sat motionless on the mossy boulder, chivalrously awaiting advances. Negeet zigzagged slowly up, landed, and they sniffed each other's muzzles.

Not for many weeks had the quiet valley rung
with such sound as stirred the forest foot that
night—whistling, clucking, snorting, and a multitude of variously pitched screams, while the two
otters swam together, darting like torpedoes across
the shallow shelves, and performing the most
wonderful loops and nose-dives in the stagnant
depths. Ye gods! they were not animals at all,
but boneless, gliding spirits evolved from the
shadows, and dissolving into the flood when so
they chose.

Spring came. The trout, still black and poorly
conditioned, rose at last from the depths and
fought their way into the sparkling shoals, while
Negeet and her mate, surrounded by abundance,
became aware of a craving for a change of food.
For days they fed on migrating eels, yet Negeet
was ever searching, listening, inclined to wander
off into the woods. One night she heard from
away up the mountainside a multitude of flute-
like notes, filling the night with the weirdest
melody that was ever attributed to the Pipes of
Pan.

Negeet had never heard the sound before, yet
instinctively she knew its significance. She
whistled to her mate and the two stole off together into the jig-saw shadows of the wood.

Away up in the rampant wilderness of the
castle grounds were two small ponds, where
stately delphiniums and white foxgloves stood
sentinel-like in the gloom. The banks were steep
and deep, overshadowed by sweet syringa bushes,
which screened an old stone seat, moss-covered

and cold, guarded by a unicorn of stone. Thither the faint palpitating sounds led Negeet and her mate, and there they fed sumptuously on the choicest of their chosen fare. Ere midnight came the banks were littered with the skins and eyes of countless frogs. The male otter, feeling in a playful mood, mounted the bank and slithered down on his front, diving with an oily swish into the pond. Out he climbed to repeat the performance. Negeet joined him, and together they rejoiced in the downward plunge, mounting, sliding, brushing aside the trailing blossoms, till soon a clean, bright slide was worn by their wet and slippery fur. Often, during the days of solitude that followed, the male otter returned alone to this quiet place and played the game which the otters played long centuries before St. Moritz was thought of.

III

Deep down among the rocks, forty yards from the water's edge and fifty yards above her favourite pool, Negeet made a nest of moss and hay, and there, late in April, her tiny cubs were born. How she loved and fondled them! How she drove her husband away with hissing snarls, though no doubt his intentions were the kindliest in the world! Husbands, however, are best away from the nursery, though only in the wild is this truth recognized.

Most uninteresting babies they really were. One was a poor, undersized little fellow, who daily

2

grew more plaintive and persistent in his calls for
his mother, till one rain-spangled evening, when
a diamond hung from every bud and twig, she
carried him out and buried his poor little remains
among the leaves. The other, his birthright undivided, sprawled in thriving helplessness while
the fairy tints of spring ripened into the fuller
shades of summer—for eight long weeks blind and
dependent, the most peevish, uninspiring morsel
of cubhood a woodland mother was ever called
upon to endure.

On the very day that the cub opened his eyes
harsh fate decreed the inevitable breach in the
united peace of his parents. Theirs had been a
happy marriage hitherto. Soon now they would
have been teaching their little one the arts of
mastery of the stream, teaching him to catch the
Miller's Thumbs among the pebbles, or to poke
his head deep into the sand after the eels, father
and mother sharing alike in the joys and sorrows
of his upbringing. But that morning there was
the sound of a brazen horn away up the river,
followed by the baying of hounds and the wavering call of the huntsman. The otter-hounds had
come at last. They had found an otter in the flat
above, and now Negeet's mate was fleeing for his
life before a score of sturdy hounds and twice as
many sturdy men.

He did not understand, of course, or he would
not have sought his mate, and thus brought the
peril to her very threshold. Now, in the hour of
his deadly need, he sought her, as he had sought
her always in brighter hours—perhaps just to

assure himself that at any rate she and her cub were safe, or because he knew no sanctuary save with her. Side by side they crouched, listening— listening, while without came the tread of many human feet, the thunderous baying of hounds among the rocks, the sharp, malicious yap of eager terriers.

" Pitter-pat " went Negeet's heart, and behind her eyes there shone two burning coals. Something was invading their home. They heard a scratching, snarling, panting sound, then a spirited little terrier, red-eyed and bristling, came squirming down between the rocks.

The male otter was there to meet him, silent, cool, but deadly intent. At a cranny on the other side, forcing an entrance from a different quarter, appeared a second terrier. Negeet spun round to face the fray, and her fury was that of a mother in despair, defending the nursling at her side.

But those terriers were grimly in earnest, recklessly intent on forcing an entrance, and the otters knew that to remain here was impossible. Negeet caught up her cub and darted by the sole remaining passage of escape, while behind her, holding the way, covering her retreat from those bristling, snapping little demons of fury, stood her mate.

He too might have fled had he chosen—fled back to the world of sunlight and of life, there to pit his skill with theirs on his own familiar ground; but, a stranger to the deadly fear of death, he chose to hold their foes at bay, while Negeet with her baby escaped by the one remaining door.

The men and women saw their otter burst
from the rocks at the water's edge, carrying something in her jaws. There was no time to act,
precious little time to think, yet some there were
who understood—understood with a pang of pity,
and who, long after, recalled the heroic little
scene—the wild mother of the waterways, battling
against hopeless odds, struggling with a load
which tried her sorely, and yet which she would
not drop. A big hound struck at her and rolled
her over. She returned blow for blow, then
catching up her cub again, glided in and out
among the rocks to the water's edge.

" Whip off the hounds! It's a bitch with her
cub!"

Too late! They were sportsmen, all of them,
and many of them were a little gentler for having
themselves gambled for life amidst bloody death,
but—there was no time. The rough going
hindered the men more than the hounds. Orders
were of no avail with the quarry in sight, and
half the pack broke away from the green-coated
whip and followed in hot pursuit.

Negeet dived, but remembering her cub, rose
instantly, then swam like a streak, glorious in her
gliding ease, towards the cauldron pool where she
had sported away so many silver hours.

Too late the huntsman saw the peril, yet had
he seen it earlier he could not have intervened.
Negeet had reached the pool edge now, still
gliding, not swimming like the hounds that pursued, and, using her whole body, not just her
paws, she headed towards the vortex of the whirl-

pool, holding her cub aloft as she swam. The hounds followed—paddling desperately, but progressing in a direction quite irrespective of their efforts. One was paddling south; he was travelling north. Panic fell upon them, and each began to lash the water into foam, rearing far out in a frantic effort to fight the flood. The huntsman last night had spoken mockingly of the power of this pool; he took it as ignorant village superstitions, but he was now to see.

Negeet reached the vortex and vanished. Down, down, she went—into the realms of dark, forbidding corridors, where the sand and gravel whirled like leaves in an autumn gale. She was fighting against time, and well she knew it. Already the cub was struggling in her grip, handicapping her sorely. Down there, jammed in a crevice, was a dim and drifting shape, tattered rags torn at by the current, with a white sinister framework showing beneath. It was all that remained of Normid, the drunken miller, who last winter had mysteriously disappeared from his village, ten miles up the river. Near to it was a pitch-black corridor among the rocks, which led upwards into the heart of the wood, thence by mysterious ways into one of those ancient clay-walled drains which have withstood storm and tempest in a manner which puts man's latest inventions in hygiene to shame. Thither Negeet headed, into that dim underworld whence no hound could follow.

The leading hound went under, and they saw him no more. Others followed, or, by chance,

were carried ashore by some force less steadfast
in purpose than the rest, while the huntsman
cursed voluminously, and the field looked blankly
on—dazedly aware that they had seen something
glorious, though a sense of tragedy and horror
possessed them all.

When dusk fell an old grey-haired angler
sauntered down to the pool, and took his seat
among the shadows to tune his tackle to the conditions of sky, breeze, and water.   Quietude
reigned everywhere, broken only by the low of
cattle and the "yap-yap" of a sheep-dog,
mellowed by distance.

Suddenly a shadow arose from the interlace-
ment of crimson and gold in the centre of the
pool, an illusive, waving shadow, part of the
common fireplay, save that it came steadily towards him with just the faintest suggestion of
sound.   It was Negeet, still carrying her baby.

The breeze was from her to the man; she did
not see him.   Now she swam rapidly to the gravel
bar at his feet, and there—at his very feet—she
laid her offspring.   Then she raised her glorious
head and looked into the old man's eyes.

Into his very eyes she looked, and his soul
writhed within him.   Was not this the irony of
fate, for that day Sam Inman had been one of the
hunters.   He had rejoiced when the hounds gave
tongue, conscious of that thrill which every true
Britisher knows at the music of the pack; and
now, back in his setting, Negeet, whom he loved
with a love the city dweller cannot perhaps understand, had laid her helpless infant at his feet.

" Negeet, Negeet! don't you know me?" he said in his quiet voice, which seemed always to bear the spell of the river. She snatched up her treasure and vanished. Between him and her there still remained the old, old barrier which neither time nor gentleness could raze.

Later that night Sam heard her calling—calling, calling for her mate. At length he answered; then the sounds drew nearer and united. All cut and ruffled he was, yet he was alive, which in the wild is all that really matters.

Later still the old angler returned home with a heart as light as in his thirteenth year, for he of all men knew that the glory of the chase is in the chase itself, and that the so-called crowning triumph is a tragedy.

THE WAIF OF PRAIRIE
HOLLOWS

That dawn Strychnine Loam, returning across
the prairie from a carousal in town, saw a jackal
skulking along the north bank of the Silvertrail
and shot it at surprisingly long range. Pelts were
of little value at this season, mid-spring, but
bounties were good—especially for *she* wolves and
jackals. When Loam rode up to his prize he was
at first gratified, then angry—gratified to find it
was a she jackal, and angry to discover that she
was nursing little ones.

The wolfer had no humane sentiments in the
matter—oh, no. To him a wolf or a jackal
merely represented a bounty, and whereas this
blunder of his meant a death of lingering misery
to the coyote's cubs, what really concerned him
was that he had cheated himself out of the possession of the whole litter. Had he known that

the coyote was nursing whelps he would have
waited in hiding for her, armed with a light rifle,
and given her a flesh wound that would maim
but not kill. Then the coyote, feeling the great
sickness upon her, would have crept to her cubs,
leaving behind her a betraying blood trail, and
the wolfer, exultant, could have tracked her to her
den, where seven or eight bounties, in addition
to that for the mother, would have been his.

Two days later young Steth Elwood, the son of
the range owner, accompanied by the ranch boss,
Lee, was riding along the Silvertrail when, turning suddenly, he was surprised to see what he
took to be a puppy scrambling over the ground on
clumsy legs in pursuit of Queenie, the fox terrier,
who accompanied them.

" Well, look at that, Lee!" cried Steth.
" Where did that little beggar spring from?"

Lee looked, and as they both drew rein Queenie
turned upon the puppy with a snarl, whereupon
the little creature rolled over in an attitude of
surrender, and Queenie was disarmed. Her heart
was soft, for at home she had puppies of her own,
but as she trotted on the little animal followed,
and the men saw it was so weak as to be scarcely
able to stand.

" Hold on," said Lee.   " It's a little coyote.
You ride south there and head him off."

The coyote whelp, however, was so absorbed
in following the terrier that it took not the least
notice of the men, so that the task of catching it
was by no means the exciting business they had
expected. Lee slipped from his saddle and called

Queenie; then, as the puppy came ambling up, looking at the man curiously, Steth threw his rope from behind, and the coyote was a captive.

It is to be feared that he bit and squealed and made Lee's thumb bleed, at which the ranch boss was all for tapping the little captive across the scalp and drawing the bounty.

" No," said Steth, " we'll take him home."

Lee looked at the boy. Like all cattle-punchers, he regarded coyotes much as one might regard a steel trap that possessed legs and ran about the range trapping anything of value to man.

" What on earth for?" he inquired. " Jackals ain't no good as pets, and I bet the boss will kick if you take him home."

" I can do as I like," retorted Steth, with an importance of person inspired by seventeen summers. " And—look here, Lee! If we put that cub in a box having an open front, his mother will come and feed him, and then we can get her, too—you savvy?"

Lee grinned.

" She'll come and gnaw him out!" the man prophesied. Then, after a moment's thought, he added: " Anyway, we can try it, Master Steth. I've got a couple of number-three traps somewhere about the outfit, and we'll go shares in the bounty."

So the baby coyote was taken back to the ranch, given some milk, and finally placed in a chicken-coop at the back of the outhouses. Steth and Lee decided not to place any traps till the mother had been once or twice, and so had over-

come her natural suspicion of this close proximity
of man, so round the coop they spread some wire
netting to prevent her gnawing him out.

The little coyote cried all night, as he had cried
with his brothers and sisters all the previous night,
but his mother never came, because she was dead.
There was only one who heard and understood
his plaintive whimperings—Queenie, the terrier;
and somehow it made her restless, rising constantly to turn round and lick her own puppies.
Once the coyote thought he got a faint whiff of
his mother, and his cries went up in a wild
crescendo. He did not yet know the scent of the
timber wolf as he came to know it later, and the
wolf, fearing some trap, decided not to go right
in and kill that wretched little coyote.

Next morning Steth was surprised to find that
the mother had not been near, so he fed the little
captive and left everything as before. The cookee
noticed that Queenie visited the coop several
times during the day, and on her last visit her
suspicion of the cub seemed to have died a natural
death, for she was seen to lick his nose through
the bars.

That evening, when Queenie was out with her
master, one of the men went with a bucket of
water and did something dreadful to Queenie's
puppies. They were all mongrels, you see, and
the regular arrival of Queenie's families neces-
sitated steps of this sort. So, when Queenie
hastened back to her brood, she found her nest
empty, save for the scent of the murderer's hands.

She searched high and low, miserably unhappy,

and at the back of her mind was a lurking suspicion that man had done this thing. Had she
possessed the faintest inkling of it she would have
hidden the puppies in that secret cache of hers,
behind the stick heap, where she hid so many of
her treasures; and now, having searched the
buildings, she went down to the Silvertrail, and
her mother sense took her to a little patch of
newly turned sand. Here she found her little
ones buried—cold, stiff, no longer a joy to her
loving eyes, and she stole away from the horrible
place, fearful of being seen in her misery, and hid
in the stick heap.

That night the captive coyote whimpered, and
Queenie listened. The sound stirred and kindled
the mother love within her, and when all was
quiet she stole out from her hiding and went to
the coop. Wire nettings and the taint of man had
no fears for her, and, forcing her way through the
barrier, she gnawed the puppy free.

Deep in the stick pile Queenie hid him, and
there for many days the little fosterling rejoiced
in undivided possession of the food that was
meant for seven. He throve apace, and his dread
of man grew in proportion. Only at night-time
did he venture from the stick heap, to sit, with
his big ears erect, his forelegs wide apart, cocking
his head from side to side as he watched the
buzzing moths and silly-bumbles.

As for Steth—he and his confederate arrived at
the most natural conclusion. The only man along
the range who could have distinguished the tracks
of the terrier from those of a wild coyote was

Strychnine Loam, the trapper, and him they did not take into their confidence. " She's been and taken him," was Steth's report, and when Lee had ambled up to look for himself his only comment was: " First time I've ever known a coyote to face wire netting."

Though the little coyote was growing rapidly in strength and staunchness of limb, his education was being sadly neglected. Had his mother lived she would, by this time, have taken him nightly on breathless mouse-hunting expeditions, and thus, lesson by lesson, he would have learned from her the things on which his success in after life was dependent. As it was he received no such training; but for a coyote he was gaining a good deal of unique experience.

A jackal is truly a creature of the wild. Keep him a captive all his life, force him into circus tricks if you like, but his fear and distrust of man will never die. Certain wiles of the chase the coyote knew by instinct, and example was not necessary in order to show him how to lurk in waiting among the sticks, then spring out at the sleek, grey rats that sometimes ventured within his domain. Silly-bumbles he caught by the score, and one day the rat trick developed into a far more exciting and perilous pastime.

A great white partridge came and sat on the stick pile and sang in a most startling and raucous manner. Coyote had seen these partridges before and knew that they were good to eat, though he had feared to venture into the yard where they lived. Now he mounted noiselessly and leaped, and the rooster vanished into the stick pile with no knowledge as to the manner of death that had seized him from below.

That evening, when Queenie came to feed him, coyote was not hungry, and the next morning found him in the same state. This was because rats had been attracted to the stick pile by the remains of the chicken, and, observing this, coyote had used the remains as a bait—carrying it into an open spot where there was nothing to hinder his pounce.

During the next few days several chickens disappeared. The little jackal became self-supporting, and Queenie began to lose interest in him. One evening one of the boys, sauntering round the stick heap, saw white feathers everywhere.

" It's the rats in the stick heap what's taking them chickens!" he reported to Lee, and Lee got to work with a number of " small fur " traps, setting them as far back in the heap as convenience permitted. " That'll fix 'em!" was his final comment, and, sure enough, it fixed the little coyote within quite a few minutes. The trap closed on one of his forelegs, and at first he simply " kia-wooed " for Queenie, thinking that something had bitten him; but, finding himself held, the instinctive terror of the trapped animal fell upon him. Dead to all pain, he dragged the trap deep into the stick heap, and there, for ten hours, fought and wrestled with it in an agony of fear and pain. Queenie went to him, but he was so fierce and red-eyed that she dare not go near. More terrible than a wolf trap was the one he had encountered, for it had tearing, cruel teeth, whereas a wolf trap is blunt and toothless.

With the early dawn the little coyote freed himself from the dreadful thing, for after all it was only a " small fur " trap, and then it was that a great suspicion of this place fell upon him. He crept out of his hiding and, for the first time, looked with interest upon the world without. The red rim of the sun was just peeping over the endless haze of the prairies. Away to the west the foothills rolled in an unending succession of light and shadow, and farther still the great dim buttes reared like cloud palaces above the haze. It was an infinite world, endlessly beautiful, breathlessly grand, and into it stole little coyote, casting fearful glances behind him as he hopped on three legs and nursed a fourth.

He was leaving the ranch for ever, but with him he took this much knowledge—that safety from man is to be found in his very midst, and that the scent of steel is the scent of *death*.

Strychnine Loam, so named on account of his alleged skill with poisoned baits, had his cabin at the cañon mouth, about five miles from the ranch, and one day, returning home with a large catch of whitefish, he left them strung under the eaves of his cabin to dry out prior to curing them for baits. Returning home hours later, he had just cast off his gear when he found that his feet were entangled in something. It was the line by which he had left the fish suspended!

All the whitefish were gone, and there, up to the very threshold of his cabin, were the tracks of a coyote—so fresh that a beetle it had trodden upon was still alive in its uncrushed portion.

The jackal must have been here when Loam rode up, and his quick senses prompted him to look about him. Was that a jackal, or was it a clump of cactus, there in the sand not twenty paces away? The wolfer did not look straight in that direction, and now he began to whistle a careless air, engaging himself by disentangling his feet. But he caught a glimpse of one bright eye shining from the inconspicuous little mound, and knew that it was a jackal.

Not ten seconds ago Loam had laid his revolver on the bench inside the cabin, and now there was nothing for it but to go and get the weapon. With a natural swing he turned in at the door, took up the revolver, and stepped out ready to use it.

But the mound was gone! Yes, that second when his back was turned had given the animal the chance for which it was watching—the chance to put the cabin between itself and the man. Loam dodged to the back, just in time to see a little cyclone of dust heading straightaway—a young, gaunt-limbed coyote that ran on three legs and nursed a fourth!

Next day, when Loam went his round, he again left a string of baits suspended upon the wall, and beneath them, hidden in the sand, were two number-four Whitehouse traps. When he came home at dusk one of the traps had been pulled out and sprung, and dirt was scratched upon the other. The baits were gone!

Strange that a coyote who had never mixed with his own kind since his helpless puppy days should grow up with all the little tricks that betray the coyotes the world over inherent in him. As a matter of fact, Lame Leg had narrowly escaped the wolfer's set, and this experience added one more stone to the temple of his knowledge—that suspended baits, though tempting, are dangerous.

A little while later Steth Elwood met the wolfer on the range.

" There's a blame little wise coyote that I can't trap about my cabin," said Loam. " Seen anything of him along at the ranch?"

The boy shook his head.

" No!" he answered; then after a moment's thought he added: " But hold on—one of the boys pegged out some skunk skins to dry. When he went in the morning something—a dog, we thought—had rolled on them and chewed up the best and finished by scattering dirt on them."

Loam laughed.

" That's a coyote trick, sure enough," said he. " Fairly reeks of coyote! What was your dog doing that she allowed him about?"

They both looked at Queenie.

" Dunno," said the boy. " She usually sends any coyote that happens along about his business, so I guess she must have been asleep."

But not even Queenie's master knew much about the night side of her character in these days—how, almost every evening, a little lame coyote would approach by the corral, thence

3

through the stick heap, to meet her at the gate.
A friendly sign would pass between them, then
the coyote would trot around as though he
owned the place. He would explore the garbage
heap, sniff round the hen-house, and trot off with
anything left lying about. Once a pair of chapa-
rajos, hanging on the bunk-house wall, were
missing when morning came, but later one of
them was found roughly buried in the dunghill.

All this time Lame Leg was collecting for himself a wonderful assortment of knowledge. The
injury to his paw was, alas, permanent, and, deprived of his speed, he was compelled to rely
more and more upon his wits. But for his intimacy
with the haunts of man he would have fared
badly in these days, for in many ways the injury
was a serious menace to him. Wolves—the big,
husky timber wolves—are to-day as plentiful in
the Silvertrail valley as when the buffalo myriads
moved north and south each spring and fall. The
buffalo are gone with the coming of man, but in
their place man has stocked the foothills richly
with herds of cattle, sheep, and goats. On these
the wolves feast, and between the wolves and the
coyotes there exists a never-relenting feud. Lame
Leg moved in mortal terror of the wolves, and it
was only because they concluded that he was as
fleet as the rest of his kind that he had managed
to survive so long.

That fall young Elwood organized a series of
wolf and coyote hunts, every dog in the locality
being mustered to the meet, whereupon the
scratch pack, with an equally scratch gathering

of hunters, would beat the sage and the juniper for any lurking vermin. In spite of the undisciplined conduct of the pack, most of the members of which seemed to regard the meet simply as a matchmaking affair, a surprising number of coyotes were killed—coyotes which, possessing the hereditary weaknesses of their kind, could not resist the temptation of running to the crest of the ridges to see what all the canine excitement was about, then yap their mockery. Moreover, those that fell did so because they trusted to their fleetness and in the end were outdistanced.

Wolves, too, were killed—one or two long-legged cubs of that year—and so were a good many of the dogs. There was one wolf in particular that gave the pack trouble—a big, gaunt, black-maned brute, whom the boys knew as Buffalo. This wolf had long mocked the efforts of Strychnine Loam, and it was this wolf that finally broke up the pack—or, rather, broke up so many of its members that young Steth found himself in the midst of a seething indignation of bereaved dog-owners who demanded compensation.

" You'll have to take it in a sporting spirit," said young Steth. " I can't pay you for your dogs, since you've had your share of the fun, but I'll tell you what I'll do. That big wolf is doubtless at the bottom of all this cattle killing, and I'll supplement the bounty by one hundred dollars to be paid the man who gets him. Now vamoose!"

They vamoosed, but the only one who went

his way with a sense of contentment was Strychnine Loam, the professional trapper of the range.

Just as there was one exceptional wolf upon
the foothills, so there was one exceptional coyote
—exceptional because he contrived to avoid the
limelight. Other coyotes might stand in silhouette
upon the hill-tops, yapping their mockery, but *he*
did not. Other coyotes might depend upon their
speed, but *he* had no speed and knew it. His
strength lay in the knowledge of his own weakness, for on hearing the pack from afar he would
sneak by the shadowy hollows away to the ranch
—would hide in the very stick heap of his nursery
days! No one thought of looking there; in fact,
the hunt generally met two miles from the ranch
and broke up an equal or a greater distance away.
Only at night-time does the truly wild coyote
come prowling round the habitation of man, and
so, at man's very threshold, Lame Leg sought and
found a sanctuary denied his abler kin.

Almost nightly Queenie saw her adopted son,
and while there were no great demonstrations
between them, each seemed content to regard the
other as a natural feature of the landscape. Then
one night when Lame Leg came he offered
Queenie an invitation to come out with him in
the most approved dog form. The invitation consisted of a nudge of the shoulder, then trotting
briskly off he would look round at Queenie to
follow. At first she was reluctant, for her duty lay
at home, but three times he came back for her
and in the end she yielded. Away up-wind he
led her, across the prairie levels where the shadows

lay like ghost-clouds, through gopher cities where the citizens sat like picket pins, then vanished backward into their burrows with " churrs " of derision as the two dogs trotted up. Once a great grey ghost-bird settled just ahead, and Lame Leg and Queenie dashed at it with chopping jaws.

The blood of the wild dog was astir in Queenie's veins, and as she trotted on her mane began to bristle and her eyes shone with the wild hunting lust. Dim and unreal the prairie lay ahead, a land of half-lights, of shifting shadows; just in front of her was her wolfish friend, and there was no sound in the vastness save the " pitter-pat " of their paws on the sand.

Suddenly Lame Leg stopped, his head aloft, sifting every breeze. A faint whiff came down the night air, faint but seductive—the delicious whiff of calf—and Queenie was for going right in here and now had not Lame Leg warned her with a growl. Up-wind he went, very cautiously, zig-zagging, yard by yard, and Queenie, who knew nothing of the perils of the coyote world, wondered at his caution. Fifty paces, thirty, twenty; then, convinced the coast was clear, Lame Leg trotted up and they feasted.

Presently Lame Leg raised his head, growled, and stole away, motioning Queenie to follow. And as they went there stole from the darkness a huge black-maned wolf, who rumbled thunder as he came; and, seated on a near-by ridge, Lame Leg yapped his mockery while the wolf feasted, and Queenie looked on with shining eyes.

That was but the first of their nocturnal forays

together, and soon it became the fashion for Lame
Leg to invite his foster-mother to any feast he
found, and for Queenie to accept.

Many dogs in wild regions adopt at nightfall
the habits of the wolf, living all day with their
masters till, at the coming of dusk, civilization
falls from them like the falling of a veil, and they
sneak up-wind, watchful, furtive, hiding from man
should he appear upon the sky-line. And as sure
as night follows day, as sure as the Snow Moon
brings her snows, their wolfish habits, sooner or
later, land them in dire straits.

One night, when the crisp evening chills had
turned to deadly frosts, Queenie, passing a pine
thicket with Lame Leg at her side, saw a prairie
chicken hanging by its head from a bough about
six feet from the ground. She looked up at it
and whined to attract the coyote's attention, at
which he rumbled a warning in his throat and
barged her with his shoulder. But the prairie
chicken smelt irresistibly good, and Queenie was
reluctant to leave it, though her companion's
growls and bristling mane forbade her touching
it.

Next day Queenie remembered the prairie
chicken. She thought Lame Leg had warned her
against it because he wanted to return for it himself, and so she sneaked off alone to secure the
prize.

Under the suspended bird, though perhaps a
yard to the north of it, was an ant-hill, now a
mound of snow, from the crest of which the bait
hung within easy reach. Cautiously Queenie

mounted the hillock, sniffing suspiciously, for she, too, had an inbred fear of traps. The crown of the mound was a likely place for a setting, but Queenie soon learned there was no trap there and climbed up eagerly, her eyes bright with the light of possession. There dangled the prairie chicken, within easy springing distance, moving temptingly in the breeze. Queenie leaped and seized it, fell back to earth with the prize in her jaws, when— thud! The trap was hidden, not at the starting-point, but at the landing, and now Queenie was firmly held by the blunt, remorseless jaws of a number-four Whitehouse!

How she fought and screamed and tussled, while no sound came to her save the mockery of the echoes! Ere long the imprisoned paw was dead and cold; she was conscious of no pain save the mental agony of being trapped. She fell to gnawing the trap, the chain, the drag—gnawed at her own imprisoned paw below the jaws, but there was no escaping from that vice-like hold.

The day died in a sullen glory of crimson— night came, but, luckily for Queenie, the frost snap had relented somewhat. But night brought its manifold terrors and shifting shadows, and the little dog crouched lower now, flattened herself to earth, and lay still in silent dread.

One hour, two hours passed by, then just be-hind her Queenie heard a sound like a human sigh. She turned, gnashing her teeth, chattering in terror, to see a big dog standing near, one paw upraised as he looked at her with savage, yellow eyes. Then, as their eyes met, Queenie's terror

died and she uttered a little whine of greeting.
It was Lame Leg, her foster-son!

The coyote circled round, sniffing the breeze.
He crawled cautiously up to the trap, sniffed it,
and backed away with bristling coat, staring at
a point just ahead. Clearly he wanted to help
her, but this was a peril with which he could not
contend. He stood with head raised, waving his
tail slowly from side to side; then suddenly he
faced up-wind, froze in his tracks, and stood
watching, listening, with terrible intentness.

Queenie crouched lower, for she, too, had
heard or seen or smelt that dreaded sign. Then
down-wind there came, so close that it was like
a thunder peal, the awful rumbling growl of a
timber wolf! Over the whiteness, full into the
starlight he came, walking stiff-legged, very
slowly, and with lowered head. His eyes shone
like awful balls of fire, saliva dripped from his
naked fangs, the huge black mane about his
shoulder-blades stood straight on end, adding
two inches to his towering stature. It was the
black-maned cattle killer on whose scalp lay the
bounty—it was Buffalo!

Did the lame little coyote steal away? No, he
stood his ground, his legs trembling beneath him,
and answered growl for growl. You who know
the coyote of the prairies will say: " That was
not a coyote trick! More likely he would slink
to the nearest ridge and yap!" But I can record
only what evidences seem to indicate as facts.
Lame Leg held his ground between the big wolf
and his helpless foster-mother, and the big wolf

paused, wondering at such audacity. Then he
charged with an awful chopping of jaws, intent
on slashing that coyote to the snow, but the
coyote was not there! And behind the very spot
where he had stood, within a yard of the trembling
Queenie, there rose from the snow a second pair
of jaws—rose with a vicious snap, like the snap
of wolfish jaws, and the big wolf fell with a roar
of terror and dismay.

He rose and shook the snow from his mane.
Terrible to behold was he in his impotence, and
now he dragged the trap from its setting, hauled
the heavy log from its scanty covering, and
with a roar turned upon Queenie to avenge his
plight.

Snap, slash, snap went the jaws of a coyote,
and the big wolf turned, his mask laid open, to
face his assailant. Queenie lay trembling and
took no part, for between her and the wolf stood
her foster-son. The big wolf charged and struck
him down, but, hindered by the trap, he could
not maintain the advantage of his nimble foe.
Snap—slash—snap went the coyote's jaws again,
a cloud of powdery snow rose up on the still air,
and the fight began.

It was a fight to a finish. For yards all round
the snow was trodden flat and smeared and
smudged with little stains of brown. " Clank-
clank " went the chain of the trap, hurled this
way and that; but the dull and slanting jaws
kept their hold. There were no witnesses of that
awful fight, save the unblinking stars and the
cowering, trembling Queenie; but the snow told

the story, told of each breathless, ghastly scene in the oldest writing of the world!

When Strychnine Loam came along in the morning he was mystified. There in one of his traps lay the terrier, shivering with cold, strain, and terror. Curled up beside her, apparently still sleeping, was a little coyote with a crippled paw, his coat gashed and rent in a hundred places. He was dead. Farther away, in the centre of that trampled ring, the big black wolf lay stretched in the snow. He, too, was dead. Of the three only the terrier remained alive, and the signs told Wolfer Loam that she was the first to fall to the traps.

Wolfer Loam was growing old. In all his experience there were many things he could not understand—things which would seem to bring the world of fangs and fur nearer to the brotherhood of man himself; yet how can we—we who know the wild dog of the hills merely as a pair of ravenous jaws prowling without in the night blackness, we who at dawn see the deeds of his bloody doing—how can we read his soul aright? Nature in her gentler moods is hidden from us by the kindly shadows our vision cannot penetrate; we see but dimly till the veil is reached, and beyond that we grope in mystery. Or if for a moment the veil be raised, then we cannot believe.

Farewell, little Lame Leg! Soon the chinook winds will blow and the valleys will be rich with budding life. Coyote will call to coyote, and from glade to cañon love song will answer love song.

But you, who in your life knew but one love, will not be here—one love which gave you life, a love all-ruling and all-conquering, blind to all blemishes, dead to all pain of self, the purest, sweetest love on earth. For such a thing you died —the only love you ever knew. Farewell!

THE FLOTSAM OF FATE

The old man sat by the garden gate in the pale evening sunshine, and watched the scene at the open mistle door with amused understanding. A family of little mongrel puppies besported themselves there in the light, while their mother, the mongrelest mixture of all mongrels—for she was a pukka sheep-dog—basked under the wall and watched her children with proud solicitude. But the object of the old man's amusement was the father of the brood, a gaunt, smooth-coated sheep-dog with big ears and bright yellow eyes, a dog as much like a dingo as any dog but a dingo could be.

Dingo did not know he was being observed, and so he had dropped his habitual reserve towards the puppies. One of them had him by the ear and a second was striving manfully to drag his forelegs from under him. The old dog was giving himself up to their gambols, a martyr to the cause, enduring it all with bored amusement, while now and then he paused to fondle and caress one of the woolly mites.

The little family scene was brought to a close by the opening of the door across the yard, and a young man came out of the house. Instantly Dingo's attitude changed. Ashamed of his condescension he began to strut away, stiff-legged and full of dignity, and when one of the balls of wool ambled after him on clumsy puppy legs, he turned with a growl and harmlessly rolled it over. The puppy returned to its mother, and secure between her forelegs it growled its puny vengeance in awful puppy thunder.

The old man laughed. " Dingo thinks a lot of them wee mites when there isn't anyone looking, Ben," he observed.

The young man seated himself at his father's side. To him the little scene had meant nothing. A good shepherd and a hard soldier he may have been, but he did not understand dogs. He regarded them much as he regarded horses—as useful just in so far as their capacity for work extended, and of no further interest. Ben Inman was known by the shepherds of the hills to possess no heart where animals were concerned, and no one liked him the better for it.

" Good dogs, too, they ought to make," the old man rambled on. " Dingo springs from the best stock in the hills. He comes from an older shep-

herding family than you and me, Ben. And Nell
—well, I reckon we could get twenty pounds for
her any day we chose. I call to mind——"

" Better get it, then," the young man answered
briefly. " I reckon nothing of her kind on these
big moors. Too short in the leg to get over the
heather."

Dingo ambled up and looked into the old man's
eyes. He did not look at Ben. Since the young
man's return to civil life he had done little to win
the favour of his dogs. The old man moved uneasily. He loved all dumb creatures in his slow
and muddle-headed way. " Sell her!" he cried
defensively. " Sell our Nell!"

But just then the woman of the house appeared
and chided the old fellow for sitting without his
hat. She said he would catch his death of cold,
which, as things transpired, was what the old
man did do. It was his third cold that spring,
and he was " getting on ". Next day the doctor
came, and went away looking grave.

Three nights later Ben was wakened by Nell
and Dingo howling in unison across at the mistle.
For some minutes he who had seen death in a
thousand ugly forms was afraid to rise, but at
length he, too, mastered his own native instincts.
The old man was dead.

The shepherds came to the funeral from far
and near, as shepherds do, looking neither so
happy nor so picturesque in their mourning garb
as in their workaday clothes; and Ben, with an
eye to the material conditions of life, did not omit
to mention that he had a promising litter of

puppies to dispose of. So, when the sorrowful
work of the day was ended, several prospective
puppy purchasers followed in Ben's wake to the
granary, where, on a fusty sack in the corner,
Nell nursed her brood.

She snarled when the strangers approached,
and forbade them touch her treasures; but Ben
cuffed her with his cap, and one by one fished
out the squirming balls for inspection. None of
the men was much impressed, for though to Nell
the loveliest things on earth, they were very
ordinary puppies. The scene was one of merri-
ment and laughter, and to the sheep-dog that was
the sore point. They had handled her puppies
roughly, and—*they had laughed at them.* Yes, they
had laughed at Nell's puppies!

Who can read the heart of the sheep-dog? To-
day Dingo and Nell had idled forlornly about the
farm. They had hated the strangers and the
whole atmosphere of extraordinary events. They
did not contemplate the future, but the present
was all significant. They had looked from face
to face, searching for one they would not find.
They knew that the man whom they had loved
and served since their puppy days would never
again fondle their ears and look into their eyes.
They knew that he was dead and that the old
beloved order now must go.

Nell's heart was heavy with strange, dim sor-
row, but now a new anxiety possessed her. Her
motherhood was the ruling factor in all her
thoughts. The men had handled her puppies
roughly and laughed at them; and in some

subtle way she knew that the future of her darlings was insecure. The one man she could trust was gone; there remained only one whom she had never come to know.

Nell went into the next room when the strangers had departed, a little dark store-room festooned with cobwebs and piled high with rusty dunnage. She had some notion in mind of hiding her puppies from the strangeness and uncertainty of it, but the prompting instinct was not quite clear. She tried to hollow out a bed on a spiky heap of mole-traps in the darkest corner of the room, but had to abandon it as not the thing she wanted. She went back to her puppies and nosed a foolish little wisp of hay over them, trying to hide them, trying the best she knew, but her poor, clumsy mother efforts merely left her with a sense of dazed bewilderment.

With the coming of darkness, the promptings of the wild dog grew in strength, and acting on impulse, she caught up one of the balls of wool and carried him whimpering into the night.

Dingo, her slave and guardian, was there to meet her. He seemed at first bewildered, but soon he grasped the general idea. They slipped from shadow to shadow together, pausing and listening. Up the stream they trotted, taking no heed of the rabbits—running flank to flank through the fragrant night shadows. When Nell's jaws ached, and she put the puppy down to rest, Dingo indicated his eagerness to take up the load, but she would not let him. She was afraid he would drop it, I suppose, which is probably what he would have done. Carrying puppies was not his department.

Through the dark ravine Nell led the way, where the shelves were draped with slender ferns, and the rolling of a pebble echoed eerily along the rocky corridor. This was a silent place, where man seldom trod, and at the head of the long defile the waters separated, so as to enclose a tiny island in their sparkling embrace—an island piled high with driftwood among the rocks.

This tiny plot of ground was sacred to Nell's possession. She had regarded it as her own since her puppy days. Here she had basked in the sun when she wanted to be alone, here she had buried her treasures in idle moments; and here to-night, deep in a nest amidst the wreckage, she hid her puppies one by one. She knew that running water all around would help to keep her secret, but alas! —her wolfish instincts, inherited from the dim ages of her wild ancestors, were half effaced, and did not warn her of foes other than such as she daily knew.

When at daybreak Ben went to the granary and found that Nell had hidden her puppies, he beat her savagely, not because she had done wrong, but because he was angry. Easily now he might have won her confidence and love, but his savage action merely kindled anew her sense of distrust and injustice. She sneaked away to her island and hid there all that day, and Dingo, willing in his boundless energy, did the work of two. " Then if she wants to hide herself she mun feed herself," growled Ben, which was only a vain

4

threat, since no one had thought of feeding the dogs since the old man fell ill.

Thus Dingo slaved all day for the master he did not love, and at night he returned to an empty food-bowl. This did not trouble him much, for with the falling of dusk the cloak of civilization fell from him, and he loped off into the night on breathless exploits.

Keeping to the hollows, never showing himself against the sky-line, Dingo made a detour when another hunting dog crossed his path; then peering over the ridge he saw a family of rabbits nibbling the grass below. Like a wild cat he flattened down and got between them and their burrow; then, quick as a hawk a-wing, he sped into their midst, and a thin-edged scream went up on the night stillness.

Civilization tends to kill all sense of fatherhood in our domestic dogs; but in the dogs of our hills, where two live together far remote from their kind, the laws of love and nature often shine forth untarnished by man's hand. Dingo and Nell partook of the habits of the wild, as do so many dogs of the ranges, and so the loftiest instincts still were theirs. Thus Dingo, hungry though he was, hastened to his lady-love with his prize and laid it at her feet.

For many days Nell did not return to the farm. Dingo lived his dutiful civilized life all day, and at night he and Nell ran wild together—wild as the red fox of the hills.

At length Nell returned, shamefaced and doubtful as to her reception. She stood in the offing with ears a-cock and gazed at the man, awaiting a friendly word, a sign, when she would grovel penitently at his feet. But Ben was piqued by the knowledge that the dog distrusted him. The thoughts and ways of the dumb creatures were a closed book to him, and so, muttering angrily, he took the rusty gun from its place in the oak ceiling, telling the woman of the house that he would " learn that dog to run away from home ".

That was exactly what Ben did do. Nell's prompting instincts warned her to flee for her life; but she took a burning charge of shot with her, and thus her whole future was sealed. She knew now, beyond all shadow of doubt, that not only would her puppies be unsafe within the reach of this man, but that even her own life could not be trusted in his hand. Nell had left the farm for good.

Ere many days were passed the news leaked out that Ben's little long-haired bitch was running wild. Old shepherds shook their heads thoughtfully and said they had known such things to happen before " when the old man died ". A lank, lean fox came down from the hills, and the poultry-yard of a neighbouring homestead was littered at dawn with the evidence of his visit. Nell was blamed. The keeper took to parading the hills at night, and one night Nell came face to face with him. There was a flash of fire, and again she fled for her life, bearing with her a stinging charge of shot. Thus Nell became an outlaw, regarding all men as her foes, a fugitive of the heather, wild as the winds that swept the

bracken slopes, a skulking vagabond of the
shadowy ways, who moved in hourly peril of her
life.

Dingo continued to live his double life. At day-
time he looked the whole world in the face, at
night a human footfall sent him bristling for cover.
He and Nell learnt the tricks of the relay chase
and the ambush; every art of the wild wolf was
known to them, but always, always they hunted
in silence. The whole wide hills, boundless under
the stars, were at their feet, and there they
roamed, spending their nights as nature intended,
endlessly free, but skulking at dawn to the places
fate had assigned them.

Nell had relinquished all claims upon and
obligations towards mankind. The laws of the
human race no longer bound her. Man had
made it clear that she was an outlaw, and as an
outlaw she was free to act and choose. But as
yet she had harmed nothing that was sacred to
man's possession. More than once she had stood,
with shining eyes, watching the fleeing sheep as
they scattered like ghosts into the night; but the
lessons of her youth bade her not to follow, and
Dingo seemed fearful lest she should. Yet she
lacked nothing of the treachery of her sex, to
which was added the far more venomous ferocity
that comes with motherhood to the creatures of
the wild, and it was only a matter of time ere
the savage life she led would tear asunder the last
of her civilized bonds.

It came in a thundery night, when the woods
were astir with the drip-drip of water, and the

very air was heavy with lifeless depression. No rabbits were astir, and Nell and Dingo had penetrated far up the valley, over the high boundary wall and into that sacred strip of forest where the keeper's cottage nestled, surrounded by the plenteous life that lay within his keeping.

In the depths of a thicket Nell stopped suddenly, one paw upraised, eyes shining, staring into the shadows of a windfall just ahead. Dingo, circling silently, got the other side of the clump, and slowly they closed.

Out of the thicket burst a mottled fawn, and well the two dogs knew that above all other creatures the fallow-deer of the range were sacred to man. They had been thrashed in their puppy days for so much as looking at them. Many a shepherd had lost his place on the great estate for carelessness which led to the destruction of the royal game.

But to-night Nell's schooling was set at naught. She was hungry, and the sight of that fleeing, bleating fawn was more than any hunting-dog could resist. The fawn dodged cleverly as Nell dashed in, then from the dripping foliage there appeared an apparition of shining eyes and stamping forehoofs—the mother of the fawn. She dashed at Nell, who doubled for her life, barely missing the savage blow that would have pounded her into the leaves, and with bristling mane and slashing fangs Dingo hurled himself upon the doe and bore her crashing to the ground.

The fawn, too, fell; then from the undergrowth there rose a second fawn, and yet another doe

rushed madly to its defence. The fighting fire
blazed from the sheep-dogs' eyes—the desire to
kill overwhelmed all other thoughts and cautions.
Systematically, savagely, they closed upon their
second quarry, till the undergrowth around was
trampled flat, and the earth was beaten black by
pounding hoofs.

The keeper, half in his dreams, heard the
frenzied barking of his dogs and, fully awake, he
listened breathlessly. Distinctly he heard the
crashing in the undergrowth, followed by the
bleating of a fawn. He arose with a chill of
apprehension and went silently out. This was
the thing that he had feared—this was why he
had dallied abroad at night-time searching for
the wild dog of the hills. Silently, swiftly, he made
his way up the mountainside, listening, pausing,
stooping, ever alert. A doe dashed by him in the
gloom, wild-eyed and terrified, then, running her
trail like hungry wolves, came two dogs he knew
—Dingo and Nell.

Two shots rang out, but the darkness baffled
him. Dingo stopped in his tracks and looked at
the man, then guiltily turned and fled with Nell
into the spangled darkness.

Dingo was not touched, but the escape had
brought home to him the knowledge of his guilt.
He knew that he had done a dreadful and un-
pardonable thing, he knew that he was doomed.
Yet he was not penitent; only he wished to hide
from man, to live to do the awful thing again.

Over the high boundary wall they sped, back
to the island at the cañon mouth. At the water's

edge they stood, staring with wonder at the flood. The stream had risen, since they left, from the merest trickle among the rocks to a roaring cataract, which bore on its racing bosom strange octopus shapes, rearing up and disappearing into the smother of foam. A bellow of thunder shook the hills as Nell plunged in. The current caught her and whirled her like a straw against the rocks of her island den. Gasping, dripping, she dragged herself out, and Dingo followed.

Only just in time, for the puppies lay in a pool of water. The surrounding cataract was rising rapidly; little brown trickles were overwhelming the island, and here and there the driftwood was already astir.

Thus Nell's mother-instincts had betrayed her. "Like to like" is the law of the wild, and the dog who turns "wolf" must sooner or later pay the wolfish price. Nell led her puppies to a loftier mound, and there, side by side, she and Dingo stood. The brown flood surged up to their very feet, the undergrowth bent beneath it, and with a roar the invading flood poured into the hollows of the island.

Nell turned to her puppies and caught up the foremost. A new fear was upon her, the fear of a power with which she could not contend. It was as though the avenging hand of God had fallen upon them in the hour of their guilt.

Dingo stood at his mate's side, willing yet hesitating; then he, too, caught up a heavy, dripping pup and turned desperately to follow her.

Nell trotted to the end of the island, carrying her load. Bravely she waded in, and boldly Dingo followed. Here the two waters met with a giddy upheaval of foam. Directly below was the dark ravine, where the flood pounded for a mile against the scowling cliffs, with many a cataract and many a whirlpool.

There was no turning back. Side by side they went their way, playing the last great game together—staunch to the end, side by side on the last fierce voyage of discovery. Whirled like straws they were swept into the central race, struggling fiercely to hold aloft their precious loads. And in the sullen twilight grey a flash of lightning touched with fingers of fire two drifting shapes, tossed like cast-off garments into the cañon mouth, to be borne away through the depths of that corridor of death.

THE COMING OF THE
CURLEWS

I

Since the old man could remember, a pair of curlews had bred annually in the patch of sheltered swamp in the corner of Black Allotment. No one knew the wild life of the mountainside better than he, who with his wife lived up there amongst it all. For years he had jotted down the arrival of the migrants, the date when he first saw trout heading up the tiny brooks, and so on; but this year he was a little worried. The curlews, his favourite birds, were a fortnight later than ever before.

For many days the river, that recognized highway of the migrants, had been pulsing with life. The first redshanks had passed ten days ago; he had seen an oyster-catcher and golden plovers galore; while the lower slopes were already alive with the cheery " Kee-wit " of the lapwings. But the curlews—where were they?

It was a matter of some importance, for to the old man spring-time was impossible till he heard the first call-note of these birds. To him it was the curlews that brought the spring, not the spring that brought the curlews. In truth, they were well on their way, and only the exceptional lowness of the river had prevented the arrival of spring a week ago. For the curlews, finding vast areas of desolate mud-flats exposed, were dallying on their way from the coast marsh-land. Usually they arrived in flocks, but this year, owing to the delay, the flocks away down the river were breaking up into packs, the packs into straggling groups, and finally the groups into pairs. And when at length the last smoky city was left behind, the little towns gave way to sleepy villages, and ultimately the blue Peninnes hove in view, the couples quietly disappeared, as couples generally do, each pair heading for some remembered spot dearer to them than any other place on earth.

Thus one evening the old man, seated on his step, over his pipe, heard a sound of laughter high overhead, of wild, piercing laughter, which seemed to bid the very hills to awaken. He jumped up with a start and almost bit his lip. " Mary!" he cried. " Mary, the curlews are come!"

Then at last he hobbled up the hillside to inspect his chicken-coops in readiness for a prospective generation of egg producers, a task he never performed till his calendar, which was surely the most unreliable of all, told him that spring had really come.

But the old man was a little puzzled. True that his favourite birds had arrived as usual to nest in Black Allotment; but one thing worried him, and he said to his friend, " William, I ain't seen no *flocks* of curlews this year. Do you reckon the fighting at sea can have harmed them?"

The other old man grunted, but ventured no comment, so our hero went his leisurely way. Twenty minutes later, when he was putting down his parsley-seed, the other old man came and leant over the gate. " George," he said, " I don't reckon it's the fighting, because I call to mind that in 1857—that's longer than you can re-member, George—there weren't no flocks of curlews, just solitary birds like what you see this year."

George grunted, and the other old man went back to his hoeing. Presently George straightened his back, relit his pipe, and hobbled after him. " William," he said, squashing a caterpillar on the wall-top, " did you say 1857? That was the spring the bridge was swept away, weren't it?"

William agreed that it was. " A terrible wet early spring," he explained; " then terrible wet all through April. The lambs——"

And thereafter the conversation wound its leisurely way through quite different channels.

II

But the curlews had come, that was the main point; and now day and night they were astir, flying, alighting, calling, cackling, hovering like gigantic humming-birds, and wheeling in mid-heaven like mighty hawks a-wing. When they rested no man could say, for the little white-walled village far below fell asleep with their wild calls ringing in its ears, and awoke with the joyous morning to hear the same triumphant notes aloft.

Whether or not all this searching and discussion concerned a suitable nesting-place one cannot tell; but if it did, one fails to comprehend the grounds for argument, for in the end the curlews chose for their nest a grassy mound which was exactly like a thousand other grassy mounds dotting the whole swamp. It would seem, how-ever, that some of these mounds were better from the curlews' point of view than others, for the hen-bird made a dozen different nests on different mounds ere her final choice was arrived at. She would scrape a hole in the ground, lie on it, sit in it, turn round a few times, then decide she didn't like it. All this time her husband looked on with uncomprehending admiration; then, grasping the idea at length, he made a nest on his own account, sat on it, sprawled over it, even went so far as to line it with grass. His wife, however, had now succeeded in that most difficult of feminine tasks—she had made up her mind; and so she stole the lining from her husband's nest to finish her own.

In due course three eggs were produced, large for the size of the bird, and of the same drab hue as the surrounding grass and ling. They were not really very beautiful to look upon, but their colour was truly serviceable, for none but a trained eye, which knew just what to look for, could have picked them out. To the curlews they were the most beautiful things in all the world.

If the birds had been restless before, they were more so now, or, rather, the male bird was, for while his wife covered her treasures he mounted guard not far away, flying from wall-top to wall-top, from boulder to boulder, or rising straight skywards on quivering wings to a point of observation, suddenly to drop like a stone to earth. Nothing escaped his unremitting watchfulness. When the shepherd-boy mounted the hill, whistling to his dog, the curlew would warn his mate by a melancholy " Toy-e-toy-e "; then, if the boy or the dog drew nearer, his notes would increase in volume, and he himself would dash from point to point, flying, alighting, screaming, screaming, till at length his mate slipped from her nest to run stooping through the grass, suddenly to rise a-wing a hundred yards away and join him, clamouring in chorus.

Thus they advertised the locality of their nest, till one day the boy turned aside and searched the marsh from end to end. Twice he passed within a few feet of the eggs, but their colour saved them even from his keen eyes, till he conveniently decided, " There ain't no nest at all."

When, a day or two later, old George hobbled up to look for the nest, the alarm of the birds was not so marked. Him they saw daily when he came to feed his chickens, and evidently his slow and quiet movements were less disturbing than the movements of the shepherd-boy. Even when old

George picked up the eggs and examined them, the curlews looked quietly on from the neighbouring wall-top with scarcely a murmur, and the old man went his way happy in the knowledge that all went well with the birds he loved.

III

The curlews were curious birds, and one of their many curious characteristics was their solicitude for others. Normally in the wild each creature cares for itself and leaves everyone else to do the same; but the curlews could faithfully be described as the sentries of the hillside. One evening the fox, sneaking down from the heather-line, was walking straight for their nest, when the male bird swooped so low as almost to lash the freebooter with his wings. The fox leapt like a flash of fire, but too late to catch that hurtling cannon-ball from the blue, and the leap carried him out of the direct line of the nest. The female crouched motionless on her eggs, and the fox did not locate her, for kind nature at this season takes all tell-tale scent from the brooding mothers of earth and air.

In the next field the old blue hare was quietly feeding. He did not see the fox creeping from tuft to tuft, till the wheeling curlew, finding his wild alarm-notes unheeded, swooped down and brushed the hare with his wings. Such a warning could not pass unobserved, and away went little Black Tips with ears a-cock, leaving Reynard to glare maliciously at the interfering bird.

IV

Old George had put some new perches in his hen-house, and that night he must needs take his lantern and hobble up to see if the fowls were using them. Unfortunately he forgot his hat, and the wind was so strong that the lantern threw long, dancing shadows everywhere. George was just about to open the hen-house door, when there was a wild scream overhead, and down came the male curlew, to dash itself at the bewildering light, then fall at the old man's feet.

"Oh, poor thing! Poor thing!" said George. He picked the bird up in his old shaky hands, but finding no hurt had befallen it, he launched it into the air again. Round and round the bird flew, screaming wildly, to dash into the lamp once more, hypnotized by the light, so that old George was compelled to extinguish the flame. He went back in the dark and, unable to see his way, walked into the swamp and got his feet wet, reaching home tired and chilled.

Next day the old man was in bed, and the day after that the doctor came to see him. George was a very old man, you see, and quite ready to go when the call came. At sundown he sat up and enjoyed his tea; then he fell asleep, with his Mary at the bedside holding his poor old hand, knotted and lined by a life of slow and honest toil.

At midnight a curlew, attracted by the candle in the room, flew twice round the house with its piercing, joyous call-note. Old George awoke. He smiled faintly. " Listen, Mary—the curlews!" he said.

To him it was the voice of spring, the voice that had brought the spring of his boyhood, of his courting youth; that had brought the spring in the quiet days of his autumn.

" Yes," said the old woman, " your curlews, George!" And she, too, smiled.

An hour later the curlew again flew round the house, settled on the window-sill, looking in at the wonderful light, then tapped three times with its bill against the glass and flew away.

But old George did not hear. He had ceased to wonder why the curlews had not arrived in flocks that year, and his Mary thought nothing strange about the happening. She, too, was very old, you see, and she knew how George had always loved the birds.

When, a day or two later, they carried old George out, to rest him in that quiet little corner where the sweet syringa grows, his wife noticed that the curlews were calling louder than ever in Black Allotment. She thought it was because of her George, for she did not know that at that very hour three little fluffy chicks had burst from their sombre shells and crept into the world of Life.

REDRIB

I

Redrib never knew his mother. He was hatched in a tiny, sandy-bedded pool away up on the heights of Bareface Mountain, together with teeming thousands of similar minute fish-life, perhaps one per cent of which would grow into adult trouthood. Early enough the weeding-out process began, and we shall see how this multitude of little fishes dwindled to the merest few ere the lush green grasses overshadowed the lower level of the burn.

When first Redrib was hatched he was, like his brothers and sisters, a perfectly-formed little fish, except that to his underside there clung a little oval bag of glutinous substance. This was the yolk of the egg from which he came, and it supplied him with sustenance for many days after his birth. Each day the appendage became smaller, and Redrib himself a little more developed and a little livelier, so that when his portable food supply gave out, he was quite well able to pick up morsels of food for himself.

Hatched in the sandy pool, along with the thousands of tiny trout, were two veritable fiends of destruction in the hideous form of the larvæ of dragon-flies. Behind a pebble one of these would crouch with tail erect like a scorpion, and when a baby trout drifted near, it pounced upon him and drained his life-blood till only the empty skin remained. At the end of a week there were dozens of empty skins washed up on the sandy shore. But one morning one of the larvæ made the mistake of striking at the bill of a drinking grouse, and was promptly hoisted ashore, while on the same happy day the other was snatched up by a dipper prospecting among the pebbles on the bed of the burn.

In a fortnight the lassitude of their extreme infancy had left most of the young trout, and though they still spent much of their time resting on the gravel bed, they were capable of yard-long darts, which served to circumvent the Miller's Thumb and most of the deadly insect life. Then came a heavy rainstorm, which swelled the burn bank-high and entirely altered the bed of it. Many of the tiny trout were swept away, many more were buried alive, and little Redrib, borne on by the tide, narrowly escaped a hundred different fates ere finally he came to rest in the deep dam of a water-trap. Vast numbers of his brothers and sisters were drawn over the weir into the underground culverts which supplied a throbbing city forty miles from this wild region. Some of these might live, to become white, wall-eyed trout, existing underground in the black, silent passages, perhaps for many years to come.

Redrib grew quickly, and by the end of June he was a perfect little brook trout, even to the red and black spots and the lustrous golden eyes. He would hang in the current under his favourite alder-bush with quivering tail and vibrating fins, pouncing upon any atom of food with the fury of a shark. Often he had colossal struggles with drifting worms larger than himself, and he would rise a dozen times at the same gauzy-winged Mayfly, till finally he wrecked it by a dexterous flip of the tail, when he and his nursery mates would tear it limb from limb.

Redrib was a born wanderer, but all his wandering tended in a downstream direction; so that by this time he was a mile below the sandy pool, at a point where the bent allotments joined the heather of the greater heights. He knew nothing of the world without—how the air was filled with the wild calling of mother curlews, mother redshanks, and a thousand other anxious mothers of earth and air. His world—the world of that tiny stream—was one complete in itself; and for everything of the world of earth and air without, there existed here an exact counterpart. The stream, too, had its hawks in the form of weird insects gliding above. True, they belonged to the surface, to the realms of air, but many of them could dive at an instant's warning and snatch their prey from the bed of the pool. The stream, too, had its stoats and weasels, which skulked among the shadows, ready to pounce upon the unwary. There was also a vast assortment of minor life, much of which was leaving the water at this season, to creep up the grass-blades, and there assume forms more wonderful and startling, leaving behind the empty husks of their aquatic days.

II

August brought a long drought, and the tiny brook dried up to the merest trickle. Soon even the trickle ceased, and there remained only a pool here and there, filled with the brightest, clearest crystal that ever percolated through a gravel bed. In one of these pools, not more than three yards long and two yards wide, Redrib was land-locked with a hundred of his friends, and, worst of all, a last year's trout, eight inches in length. They were in little danger of starvation, for flies were plentiful, but the unnatural condition of things brought about many a real menace in other ways. To begin with, the last year's trout turned cannibal and hid in a shadowy nook, which he never left except to dart upon some unwary mite that drifted by. He would doubtless have accounted for all of them had not two wild-cats, the sole survivors of their kind in the district, taken to hunting the burn at this period. One day they appeared on the bank, glowering down into the water with vicious yellow eyes. The little trout knew instinctively that the felines were dangerous, and Redrib, wise in his generation, immediately hid under a pebble and " nuffin " said.

One of the cats crouched at the narrow neck of the pool, while the other walked along the bank and drove the frightened fish under the very nose of his waiting accomplice. The yearling's nerves gave out, and he darted from his hiding, to be scooped into the air by one lightning sweep of the crouching feline's forepaw. Three other trout were caught ere the cats left the pool —two of them being grovelled from under the bank by the groping forepaws of the fur-clad anglers.

Some of the little trout died of fright after this adventure; several more were swallowed by a kingfisher; and the owls which, like the cats, had taken to hunting the burn as its waters dwindled away, accounted for so many of Redrib's friends that when the rains came there were scarcely a dozen of them left. It is thus that nature's whole balance is upset when man steps in. For ages past the trout had deposited their spawn in this burn, and so long as there was water enough in winter for the spawning fish to reach their recognized " redds ", they would continue to do so. Yes, even though that distant city stole all the summer supply and left their children stranded in pathetic little ridges among the pebbles.

At length, with the veering of the wind, there came a mighty flood, and Redrib, now strong enough to battle with it, swept joyously down-stream, feasting as he went, till he reached a still, shallow stretch of water with a bed of silver sand. In this loch were flashing multitudes of little trout, not one of them more than eight inches in length. It was the nursery of the spawning-brook, for, being only two acres in area, and nowhere more than three feet in depth, it offered no attraction for larger fish. So here Redrib rested a while, feasting and splashing with his fellows, and nowhere in all the world was a merrier, safer nursery than the loch of silver sand.

III

The autumn faded by, the water became icy cold, and Redrib spent most of his time under a flat boulder, not exactly hibernating, but some-what torpid. This was part of nature's scheme of protection, for now there began to appear many adult trout, all voyaging up into the hills as Red-rib's mother had voyaged the year before. Many of them were mammoth fellows, black, gaping leviathans; and though all were obsessed with the desire to travel, the old bulls would have played sad havoc in Silver Loch but for this period of winter torpor which caused the tiny fish to hide.

When April came Redrib was a fine yearling trout of seven inches in length, and now, with the desire to travel once more upon him, he threw in his lot with a devil-may-care band of youngsters at the tail-end of the adult procession passing downstream. So Silver Loch was left, and down

over many a sparkling weir, across many a deep
and shadowy pool, Redrib and his mates splashed
their scintillating way. In one of the pools he had
a narrow escape, for suddenly from the depths
below there rose a strange, wavering shape.
Straight at the little trout it came, a hideous,
writhing, serpent form, but luckily for Redrib,
he kept his head and did not attempt to aspire
to the heights of a flying-fish. He darted to left
and right like a startled snipe. The little fellow
nearest him, who made for the surface and
jumped, fell back into the jaws of the eel, and
there his history ended. Thereafter Redrib knew
that when travelling strange waters it is best to
keep to the edge and avoid the shadowy depths.

Another month of idle travelling brought little
Redrib to yet another loch, this time a noble sheet
of water of profound depth. The name of the
loch is Dungeon, and on its mighty rocky shores
the peregrine and the buzzard have their nests,
hidden from the four winds by nature's towering
buttresses. Dangers enough had beset Redrib's
voyagings hitherto, but they were as nothing to
the dangers that existed now. Here he could
never have survived his helpless infancy, and thus
we see the wisdom of the guiding instinct which
takes the mother-trout away into the tiny springs
to lay her eggs, where the little ones will be safe
at any rate from the greatest of their foes, their
own kind.

Redrib arrived in Dungeon just in time for the
Mayfly hatch, and during the days that followed
the surface of the loch was literally brown with

gauzy-winged life. All day Redrib, with armies of his fellows, rose and splashed along the shallow margins, gorging to repletion, then wrecking flies for the fun of the thing. Redrib grew at an alarming speed, and his dashing energy would have been bewildering to watch. He took an immense joy in being alive, and very often he tried his strength with his fellows. In one of these fights he got his jaws interlocked with those of another fish of the same size, and thus they struggled till the other fish, the weaker of the two, became limp and unresisting. Then Redrib struggled hard to swallow him. Of course, it was impossible, since they were both the same size, but for ten minutes Redrib persisted, till the other fish was torn and bleeding. This contest, which was waged for the possession of an insect turned from under a pebble, had the effect of influencing the whole of Redrib's future career.

Though the small fish kept to the shallow water of the loch margin, the night was a veritable horror to them, for with the coming of darkness there rose from the shadowy depths many a big black raider to feed upon the narrow shelves. More than once a movement in the water warned Redrib to skedaddle for his life, and, glancing round as he darted off, he would see a pair of mighty gaping jaws with hooked teeth pursuing him, and two savage golden eyes of horrifying size sweeping towards him through the blackness. Once he was driven ashore by one of these giants of his own kind, and there this story would have ended had not a friend appeared in the disguise

of a mortal foe. Redrib was drifting idly when
his mammoth relative rushed at him from the
depths, and Redrib, having cleverly dodged,
made, as usual, for the shallow water, where the
big fish would be at a disadvantage. But the
cannibal trout persisted, rushing along with tremendous noise, his broad back out of the water,
till Redrib, darting and dodging, found himself
suddenly high and dry on the gravel bank. And
there he struggled and gasped, while his adver-
sary lingered not a foot away, watching him
fiendishly. Another kick and Redrib would have
been between those awful jaws, but at that very
instant the grey post standing near suddenly
transformed itself into a bird. Two big grey
wings wafted the air, and with one sedate and
ungainly hop the heron reached the spot. A
lightning stab of the bayonet bill, and the big
fish, impaled through the eyes, was dragged and
jerked up the gravel bank, leaving behind a
streak of crimson on the crystal flood. And while
the heron strove to swallow the mammoth of the
depths, good luck and gravity, rather than sound
judgment, took Redrib back to his natural element.

Other narrow escapes Redrib underwent ere
the cold and leaden touch of winter settled upon
the mighty loch. Once one of the party of cor-
morants, which had their stronghold on the
lonely island in the centre of the loch, pursued
him hither and thither till his breath gave out,
and it was only because a perch, no longer than
himself, but a good deal heavier, dashed out to

swallow him, and itself got swallowed, that he managed to escape.

But Redrib's enemies became fewer and fewer as he himself grew. Once he fed with gusto on the larvæ of a dragon-fly of the kind he once had dreaded, and now he found that when he erected his dorsal fin and opened wide his jaws, the smaller fish fled from him towards the shallow water. He no longer frequented the extreme edge, but moved with the medium weights between the sunny shallows and the murky depths; but it is to be feared that very often now he voyaged shorewards, and returned a few seconds later with a little pink tail showing between his jaws.

IV

That winter Redrib mated with a female trout of his own size and age, though she was smaller in the head and more rotund of figure. Together they journeyed up the burn to Silver Loch, sometimes struggling for hours, till completely exhausted, to mount a rocky shelf, but always in the end their efforts succeeded. On and up they voyaged, obsessed by the one desire to gain some distant point, and though it is not to be expected that Redrib should recognize the place, their voyagings at length ceased in the very pool where he was born.

Here the female trout got busy making her nest, which she did by nosing away the gravel in a long groove running lengthwise with the stream. In this groove she laid her eggs, covering them with sand by the movement of her big underfins; while Redrib helped at intervals by nosing the piled-up ridge back into place. The fertile eggs were sticky, and stuck to the bed of the pool; the infertile ones drifted away so as not to foul the redd. When the whole batch was safely harboured, the adult trout turned downstream again, their parental duties faithfully and fully accomplished.

At Silver Loch Redrib dallied for a while, and the criminal tendency, which had showed evidence at so early an age, now rapidly developed. He was fiendishly hungry, and for days he wrought the most appalling havoc among the small fry of the nursery loch. Early spring found him still there, a wolf in the sheepfold; and when, finally, he decided to proceed on his leisurely way, he found the exit of the loch so shallow that he decided not to trouble. And so he remained in the nursery loch till a heavy spate in late summer fairly carried him out, and down to Dungeon Loch he went.

If any further influence had been needed for the framing of Redrib's future, that period in the nursery loch decided it. All trout are cannibals more or less, but the trout that settles down to live exclusively on its own kind soon comes to bear, in every line of its being, the brand of the cannibal. That summer Redrib's head and mouth grew enormously. True, he put on weight all round, but the development of his upper parts was out of all proportion. He took to hiding in the deep waters, seldom stirring during the day, and at night ranging the shallow shelves like a frenzied tiger. The result was that the gold and silver left his flanks, which partook of the murky gloom of the deeper waters. No longer a creature of the sunshine, no longer a joyous nerve of life in the dancing, sparkling spray, we leave him now for a while to the sombre depths in which so many of the mysteries of his life were hidden.

V

Few wild creatures, whether of earth or air or water, die by the natural course where they have lived. Sooner or later, when their prime is past, there comes the call to wander off; and twelve years after the day that a tiny bright-eyed brook trout glanced and flashed from the loch of silver sand towards the great world of the lower loch, a mammoth black trout sallied forth from the depths of Dungeon on a last fierce voyage of discovery. Men would have told you that this creature was of the black loch species, and had you said, " This is a common brook trout," few would have agreed.

Redrib was now an eight-pound fish, but had he been perfectly proportioned he might have scaled twenty. His head and his fins were huge; his tail would have been huge, but that the lower half was worn away by constant contact with the floors of the gloomy recesses. Down from the loch to the river he went, travelling once more through sparkling, flashing water, down, and still down, amidst drifting blossoms, till the hills were left behind and green meadows spanned the valley. More than one angler he encountered *en route*, leaving them gaping at their tackle, himself hardly aware that a hitch had occurred. So in due course the meadows, too, were left, and the river wormed its dark and oily course between the grey walls of a city.

A row of little urchins sat with dangling legs at the quayside, fishing for the swarms of minnows invisible in the depths below. One of them, more ragged even than the rest, with a willow wand for a rod and a length of string for a line, suddenly scrambled to his feet with a frightened shout, clinging to his primitive tackle .with trembling fingers.

Redrib had seen the swarm of little fish, drawn by the common attraction of the line of baits, and dashed into their midst out of sheer ferocity. All of them scattered but one, which was in the embarrassing predicament of having just swallowed the urchin's bait, and him Redrib swallowed with a snapping and a worrying of mighty jaws.

By some whimsicality of fate, there was no flaw in that urchin's tackle. The string was sound, the knots were good, the small-eyed hook refused to snap. Steadily, remorselessly, Redrib was drawn to the top, lashing the water into foam, and two loitering bargemen lent a willing hand in sealing his ignominious fate.

Thus, washed up with the dregs of the human city, filtered with the driftwood to the outside edge of the loch of men and women, he who had been great among the small, a despot of the depths, fell to the smallest and least, the humblest of all human anglers. But about the silver bed of a lonely little loch, away back in the hills, there sported a new generation of yearling trout, each weaving its own life-history—a fabric of bright and scintillating shades, in the making of which the turning of a pebble, like the breaking of a thread, might decide the texture for good or ill, a thing of coarseness or of beauty incomparable.

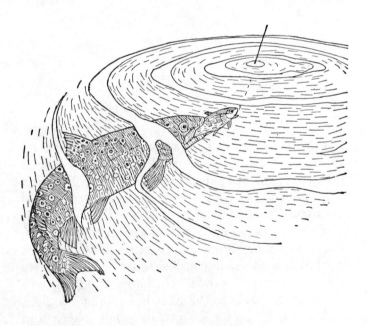

THE DEATH-LEAP

I

Fireflank, the fox cub, sat under the silent stars in the big white world and listened. He had come far and fast, and he was hungry, yet upon him rested the fear of the unknown, for this country was new to him.

Eight days ago Fireflank had left the green fields and pine-woods of his native land, had left his father and mother and sisters and brothers, to seek fortune on his own. He had turned his steps northwards towards the blue hills, loping, loping, mile after mile, sneaking into cover where and when the dawn found him. He had eaten little during this late autumn migration, for he was afraid, horribly afraid of the foxhounds that had chased his sister and him, and had finally pulled his sister down—though he did not know it—within sight of their nursery home. So Fireflank, alone, homeless, had fled into the heart of the mountains, where this peaceful winter evening found him; and here, among the loose rocks of the Garolgome Wood, he had already half decided to make his home.

He sat under the silent stars, I say, at his den mouth, his big ears acock, daring himself to sneak down into the valley towards that white-walled homestead across the river. An hour ago he had heard the honking of geese and the cackling of poultry, from away over there, and also the barking of a dog. Fireflank was very young, or he would have waited till after midnight; but now his hunger led him on, and down towards the noisy river he stole, sneaking in and out among the hazels till he reached the bank. The thunder of heavy waters filled the air, the trees at the river edge were all bearded and caked with frozen spray, but, leaping from rock to rock, where a false step might have meant disaster, Fireflank gained the other side. The idea of having the river between the region of his nightly raids and the place that he already called his home appealed to his native instincts.

There was a light in the farm window, but also there was wafted on the still air a delicious whiff of poultry. Fireflank kept his eyes upon the light. It seemed to draw him. When far out in the centre of the field he saw the farmer and his family seated over their supper. The fox cub

6

snarled a silent snarl, then, making a detour, he got to the back of the farm buildings whence came the scent of fowl and sneaked in under the orchard gate. All was white and silent, and there —oh delight!—sat five plump roosters, huddled together on the branch of a plum tree not twelve feet from the ground!

Fireflank drifted under the branch and looked up with shining golden eyes. The fowls moved uneasily, and their movements seemed to excite him. He yapped twice, two sharp, metallic "yaps", and the foolish roosters, instead of sitting tight, began to edge out towards the end of the already overstrained branch. "Yap-yap!" said Fireflank, louder now, for in his excitement he had forgotten the farmer and his dog. "Yap —Yap—Yap!"

One of the roosters fluttered, began to lose its balance, and then, flapping weakly, slowly subsided backwards till it swung head down, in the most absurd manner imaginable, still hanging on frantically by its feet. Fireflank fairly yelled with glee, making desperate little jumps, though he knew it was only a matter of time ere the rooster fell to meet him.

At that instant the farmer rose from his supper. "Whist-ye!" he muttered, threatening to cuff one of his boys; then he held up his hand in a gesture for silence. All of them listened. The dog, basking before the peat fire, pricked his ears and assumed an attitude of intentness. "Yap—Yap! Yap—Yap—Yap!"

"Thond's a fox!" said the farmer in an excited

whisper. He snatched his gun from under a rafter, his dog was at his side, and as he opened the door he whispered, " Fix him, Nell!"

Nell shot silently forth, for she knew as well as anyone what was amiss. The word " fox " was associated in her mind with many a breathless chase in the spring of the year, when she and her master slept out on the hills to guard the newly-born lambs, and Nell knew the ways of mountain foxes. So she stole silently out, swift as an arrow, intending to take the thief by surprise.

" Yap—Yap!" yelled Fireflank, and at that moment the branch on which the fowls sat gave an ominous creak and broke. Down came a veritable avalanche of chickens, each so dead with terror that it fell like a stone, and Fireflank found himself the centre of a hailstorm of descending riches. They landed in his face, on his neck, on his back, and like a little cyclone he whirled this way and that, sending up a cloud of powdery snow, and dealing death at every snap.

Over the high boundary wall appeared a shadow, and had not Fireflank been too busily occupied he would have seen a vision of bristling hair and naked fangs bearing pell-mell upon him. As it was, he did not see Nell till she actually collided with him, rolling him over and over amidst a maelstrom of chickens, cutting his shoulder with her fangs. But Nell overshot and was too slow in turning. In an instant Fireflank was up, darting like a streak of light for the gate through which he had come. He wriggled under it, and Nell, at his very heels, collided heavily

with the bars, for the space was too small for her
to follow. She lost two priceless seconds in at-
tempting it, then lost two more in scrambling
over the wall. Away went Fireflank, floating
easily over the snow, keeping to the shadow of
the wall, and heading back towards the river,
while the farmer strove in vain with his rusty
muzzle-loader to get a line on the drifting
shadow.

The sheep-dog was fast, and at the very river
margin, as Fireflank was about to cross, she
turned him—oh fruitless triumph!—forcing him
to run downstream. Fireflank knew he could
throw her off among the loose rocks of Garolgome Wood, so cross the river he must at all
hazards.

His chance came, and he took it. At the very
brink of the fall, where the entire waters of that
wonderful river topple over a cliff fifty feet in
depth, there is a single pointed boulder protruding above the angry flood, and to-night the
surface of that boulder was sparkling with ice,
affording scarcely sufficient foothold for a fly. It
was a tremendous leap for a young fox, but for
Fireflank it was neck or nothing. He floated out
across the angry flood, seemed scarcely to pat
the boulder with his dainty paws, then floated
on and up, up into the shadows of the friendly
Garolgome.

Nell also leapt, but the boulder was pointed
and coated with ice, as I say. Immediately below
was the whirlpool, into which whole trees sometimes vanished to come up as splintered drift-wood.

High up in the wood, at the mouth of a crevice among the rocks, all draped and festooned with masses of moss and the dead fronds of ferns, Fireflank sat with lolling tongue and listened. His pursuer was gone! Some minutes later the fox cub stole down to the water's edge and looked. She was not there! He chased his tail a round or two, crossed the river higher up, stole into the orchard and picked up the plumpest of his kill, while two fields away he could hear the farmer calling for his dog!

It was late that night when the man returned, silent and heavy-hearted. Something at the mistle door attracted his attention; it was Nell's food-bowl, filled with dirt scratched up from under the snow and scattered broadcast. The man knew the sign as that of a fox's uttermost contempt, and as he swore heavily under his breath there sounded across the distance Fireflank's " Yap—Yap " of mockery.

II

Sweepingly triumphant though his first raid had been, Fireflank had sense enough not to visit the farm a second time. It was too near his home in Garolgome Wood, and during the nights that followed he made several similar raids on other farms, far distant from his own home and located on the ranges of other foxes. In this manner he came to know the gaps in the walls, the gates with the narrowest bars, the drains and the swamps, all of which were endlessly useful to him in the way of baffling the clumsy sheep-dogs.

One day, when all was very quiet, Fireflank stole from his subterranean dwelling, and fell to amusing himself by tearing the bark from a dead tree, in order to nose out the insects hibernating beneath it. Presently a movement near by attracted his notice, and looking up he saw another young fox standing quite near with ears acock, eyeing him inquiringly. Fireflank uttered a rumbling growl and his mane stood on end, but the newcomer did not stir. Fireflank moved to the windward side to get the caller's body scent. Both seemed satisfied, and they approached in attitudes of armed neutrality to sniff each other's noses. Thus introduced, they considered themselves on terms of discussion, and half an hour later, strange to relate, the two solitary little dog foxes were curled up together in Fireflank's den, sharing each other's warmth.[1]

Whence Goldeye had come I do not know, but he proved to be the most warm-hearted, silly-good-natured little fox cub that ever poked his muzzle into a cold mouse hole. The two young foxes now took to hunting together, and ere their strange partnership was a week old it all but culminated in a tragedy for one or both of them. It happened thus.

With intermittent breaks the Frost King still held the country in his iron grip, and Fireflank and Goldeye, hard pressed for food, one night

---

[1] This is founded on fact. Bachelor foxes have been found living together with the same apparent devotion for one another as mated couples.

H. M. B.

stole through the high boundary wall and out on
to the moors above Garolgome. Here the snow
lay in deep drifts among the crags. There were
blue mountain hares and red grouse in the
heather, but the foxes were after nobler game.
They paused on a ridge and sniffed the icy wind.
It bore to them a strange scent, like the scent of
sheep, only more potent. It was the scent of the
half-wild goat herd that dwells to this day among
the crags of the Redstone Rigg.

Goldeye showered his kisses on Fireflank's nose
to indicate his eagerness, then silently up-wind
they stole, keeping to the hollows, never showing
themselves against the sky-line. There were the
goats, gathered in a space among the crags,
twenty or thirty strong, comprising mothers with
their kids and one enormous billy who possessed
towering, upsweeping horns.

Hidden in a hollow, the two foxes decided upon
their plan of campaign. Goldeye was to dash
right in—which was just his mark—looking as big
and terrible as possible, and thus, having scattered
the herd, Fireflank would single out one old
nanny and keep her occupied, while Goldeye
drove her kid down the slope away from the rest
and thus made sure of it.

Goldeye carried out his instructions to a nicety.
He stole up unseen to within a few paces, then
dashed out towards the goats, bristling and snarling. They, for their part, should now have
scattered like chaff before a cyclone, but they
did nothing of the sort. Every nursing mother of
the clan calmly got up and sniffed her kid. It

FIREFLANK LEAPS

88

was the most perfectly orderly scene imaginable. The billy also got up, shaking his noble head, stamping his forehoofs, and glaring at the fox. Then, in a most unperturbed manner, without panic, even without haste, the whole herd, led by a disreputable old nanny, trickled out along a narrow shelf running across the face of the precipice to the north. The billy held the way till all were gone, then with dignity he followed.

Once on the shelf the goats began to move, running in single file—drifting like a string of ghosts along the black face of the crags, while the rumble of hoofs filled the air. " Chase them!" yapped Fireflank, and suiting the action to the words he bounded out along the shelf in hot pursuit, Goldeye, yapping wildly, at his heels.

The shelf was scarcely two feet in width, and below them was a black fall through space almost sheer to the valley. Pell-mell along the perilous path the two young foxes ran, till they reached a point at which the mountainside jutted out, the trail beyond it invisible, and here, just round the corner, that fearless old billy was awaiting them. Fireflank was face to face with him in the twinkling of an eye. Down went those sweeping horns, and with a snort the old warrior dashed to the fray.

Another second and Fireflank would have been swept to his doom, but in that narrow interval of time he saw a protruding boulder jutting out from the face of the cliff twelve feet below. He made a desperate leap for it, and, as he left the shelf, the battering-ram of bone and muscle hurtled past him, filling his eyes with dust. Gold-eye had already turned back and was fleeing for his life, so, glaring and shaking his head at Fire-flank, now secure below, the billy plunged on into the night after his harem.

Fireflank glanced about him. Only a young and foolish fox would have found himself in such a predicament, for there he was, perched dizzily on a pinnacle protruding from the sheer face of the precipice, gloomy space beneath him, night on every side, and positively no way up or down. He saw immediately that he was a fixture, and remain here he must, until, pressed by hunger, perhaps, he might nerve himself to making this risky and wellnigh impossible leap back to the shelf. He began to whine pitifully, at which Goldeye came back and peered down at him, seeming to think his predicament an immense joke. He yapped in mockery, while Fireflank growled thunder, and eventually Goldeye saun-tered off, leaving him to his fate.

But with the first streak of dawn Goldeye was back. All ridicule had left him now; he whined anxiously, and had there been a way down he would doubtless have descended to Fireflank's side, which was the sort of silly thing he would do. When daylight came he sneaked off into the heather near, overlooking the imprisoned Fire-flank, and curled himself up there.

Some hours later two peregrines spied the stranded fox and came hurtling down from the clouds, screaming savagely, and apparently in tent on driving Fireflank over the edge with their lashing wings; but Goldeye dashed out along the shelf and stood above his friend, fangs gleaming, mane on end, and the peregrines planed and looped and corkscrewed back into the clouds.

The wretched day passed, night came with cold, driving sleet, and the noble little Goldeye, himself lean with hunger, appeared on the shelf above, carrying a blue mountain hare. He dropped it to his mate and Fireflank caught it, feasting hungrily.

Again the cold grey dawn stole across the valley, and then, from away down the corrie at the foot of the crag, there sounded the barking of dogs. There was silence, then the dogs appeared at the foot of the crag, coming in this direction, and with them a man with a gun—a game warder. Foxes are not protected in these wild hills; in fact they are shot and trapped whenever possible.

Fireflank crouched low in terror now, while Goldeye watched anxiously from his outlook near. To them the appearance of the man and dogs could mean but one thing—that the imprisoned Fireflank was seen, and they were coming to destroy him. Steadily the three approached, the man constantly pausing to peer up the face of the crags—looking for the peregrines really, though the foxes did not know this. They knew only that it was a time of mortal peril, and it was then that Goldeye did a very noble thing, which many a fox has done to save its cubs, but few have done to save one of their own kind who was merely a friend. He stole cautiously out to

meet the man and his dogs, to lead them off in
pursuit of himself and so save Fireflank.

Thus the keeper was suddenly surprised to see
a little red fox loping across the open space just
ahead of him in full view of the dogs; but alas
that Goldeye had never learnt the exact range of
firearms! The keeper carried a long-barrelled
ten-bore gun, charged with number three, and in
an instant little Goldeye was aware of stinging
pains all over his body, as though a swarm of
hornets had attacked him. He yelped and
doubled his pace, not mortally wounded though
he was peppered all over, and behind him came
those two iron-limbed missiles of death, schooled
in all the lore of mountain foxes, and nursing a
bitter feud against their kind.

Fireflank, on the pinnacle above, watched the
opening of the chase—saw the two hounds closing,
closing, while Goldeye, limping as he ran, and
leaving little spots of blood upon the whiteness of
the snow, headed for a sheep-hole in the wall and
vanished.

Did Fireflank understand? Did he realize that
his friend was gambling with death on his behalf?
Be that as it may, the sight of the chase excited
him, seemed to make him desperate, and he
forgot even his terror of the man.

Thus the keeper, looking up the face of the cliff,
saw what looked like a sheet of brown paper
caught by the wind and beating against a shelf,
till he realized that there was no wind. Then he
heard a yelp and realized that what he saw was
a fox, leaping desperately to gain the goat-track,

leaping and falling back again and again, in mortal peril of sliding to its doom. The range was too great, and the keeper stumbled towards a nearer point; but as he went he saw the fox gain a hold with its forepaws on the extreme edge of the shelf, and writhing, struggling madly, haul itself up till its hindpaws gained a hold, and so on to safety. In a moment it was gone, racing along the shelf and into the heather, and the keeper swore softly.

Yet he knew he had seen a noble thing. He had seen a fox risk everything to save its mate, crag-bound on the shelf above.

Goldeye, in the meantime, hard pressed by the dogs, was making desperate efforts to regain Garolgome Wood, but each time he headed in that direction one of the dogs headed him off. His tongue was lolling now, his steps lacked their buoyancy, and every here and there more crimson spots on the snow told the tragic story! The trees seemed to sway before his eyes, a mistiness enveloped the trail ahead, and goodness, how weary he was! His limbs ached, his brain throbbed, a burning thirst racked his throat, yet just behind him were those red-eyed snarling dogs, ready to tear him asunder. Once he fell; it was at the crest of a deeply washed watercourse, and one dog was upon him in a trice. Down they went together, over the edge, rolling and sliding down the almost perpendicular bank of moving shale, to land with a thud and split asunder among the rocks sixty feet below. The fox fell lightly and was up in an instant, but the

fall shattered the breath out of the dog and left
him panting. Goldeye headed tottering down the
rocky bed of the creek, at which the second dog
came tobogganing down the bank of shale in
savage, bristling pursuit.

Goldeye tottered. Could he make it—no! No!
His own life's blood, teeming from a wound in
his scalp, got into his eyes, his heart was thump-
ing like a trip hammer, and behind him, not ten
paces behind, came the leading hound. At the
foot of the gorge, fifty yards ahead, he decided to
turn at bay, to stand and fight for his life to the
bitter end.

But as he neared this point there was a flash of
gold and russet, and there, behind a windfall,
stood Fireflank, white-fanged and prepared—a
waiting, bright-eyed little fighter, ready to meet
his foes on their own ground—ready to dare death
on his friend's behalf. Goldeye slipped weakly
past him, then as the hound came dashing up,
Fireflank shot from his retreat like a bursting
shell. His big tail struck the hound across the
eyes, momentarily blinding him. Snap, click,
snap went Fireflank's jaws, and the dog, thrown
from the trail he was running, turned with dripping muzzle to face his assailant.

But Fireflank was up and away, sliding under
the windfall, gliding in and out among the rocks,
both hounds, bellowing their hatred, following by
sight. Away down to the river he led them, then
across from rock to rock, through the poultry
yard of the farm he knew, scattering the hens
like chaff, then up a little-frequented valley that

led to a land of dead and abandoned lead mines in the heart of the Bentland Heights.

Fireflank was running easily, but for the hounds it was the stiffest chase they had ever known. Now and then the fox seemed almost within reach, then suddenly he would slide through a gate with bars so narrow that the dogs bruised their backs and their shoulder-blades trying to wriggle after him. Once he skimmed daintily down the sheer mountainside, leaping from rock to rock, but his heavy pursuers, hard behind him, set a veritable avalanche moving, and were almost annihilated by the crashing boulders. At the foot of the slope the fox looked round and leered at them, then down the valley again, back the way he had come, towards the river and the friendly Garolgome.

There was a breath of icy wind, the snow-flakes began to fall, blotting out all objects thirty paces away. Through the whirling whiteness Fireflank ran, decoying on his pursuers, ready now to lose them in the blizzard, for his breath was giving out. Then harsh fate dealt a stunning blow to the hunted fox, robbing him, in the moment of triumph, of his glorious gifts, for, leaping the wall and landing on the high-road near the farm, Fireflank trod on something—on a pointed spike of glass, buried in the snow. It passed clean through his forepaw, all but stunning him with pain, and hearing his yelps the dogs redoubled their efforts, drew in behind him, encouraged to the utmost of their speed by his close proximity.

On three legs now, scarcely able to hold his

own, sick with pain, panting for breath, Fireflank headed for home—straight and true, knowing that life lay in that direction only. He gained the river bank with not a yard to spare. He felt the hot breath of the hounds on his flanks and knew that they would catch him ere he could get across. Then he remembered another chase, glorious in its triumph. Quickly he turned and dashed downstream—down along the grassy bank till the thunder of the falls filled the air.

The single rock in midstream was covered with snow to-day, but beneath the snow was a coat of ice. Fantastic ice formations festooned every rock and clung in clusters from every beard of moss. Fireflank leaped, using his wounded paw and leaving a crimson imprint—he leapt and landed, light as a thistle-seed, buoyant as a russet leaf of autumn, landed and fled on towards the rocks of his secure home.

The hounds did not falter, and through the whirling whiteness they too leapt for the pointed rock in midstream. Instantly the first lost his foothold, clawed desperately for a moment, but was caught by the tide and whirled away, uttering the cry of a dog which knows itself doomed. Unwaveringly, fearlessly, the second also leapt, gained a footing, slithered back, clawed to the top, slithered over into the current, lashing the water into foam. And it, too, was drawn over the brink of the fall, to be shattered lifeless among the rocks, caught by the eddies of the whirlpool, sucked into its vortex, and so, beaten and pulped, to become the sport of the waves.

Long after darkness had fallen the voice of a man could be heard along the river bank, calling, calling for his dogs as he searched the whirling whiteness. The snow had covered all signs, yet he could guess what had happened, and it was only the stubborn Celtic blood in his veins that bade him continue the search long after all hope was relinquished. He knew that his dogs had been decoyed to their doom, he knew that he would never see them again, yet far into the night he searched. And when at length he turned his steps wearily homewards he heard from the heart of Garolgome Wood a mocking " yap-yap ", which told him that he and his dogs were the sport of the wild creatures they had designed to kill.

THE FOREST OF HIDDEN
RUNWAYS

It was " bedding night ", and bedding night
in the badger warren, let it be clearly understood,
is no end of an affair. Ten minutes after the last
golden beams of the setting sun had cast a de-
parting ray across the fir spires, the whole badger
family—consisting of father, mother, and four
cubs—had turned out, though this turning out
process was a matter of time. First of all father's
grizzled muzzle appeared at the mouth of one of
the big main burrows, poked inquiringly this way
and that as he sniffed the breezes, then backed
in again. Next, mother's muzzle appeared within
the shadows of another entrance, and thereafter
at each of the main burrows the two appeared in
turn. Since the occupied portion of the warren
comprised at least half an acre of ground and
had no less than sixteen entrances and exits, it

will be understood that these preliminaries took time.

At length the head and shoulders of the old male badger appeared, and emerging snail-like he sniffed the damp earth within the radius of his nose, licked up an earwig that was indulging in a long-distance cross-country steeplechase; then, as a beetle dropped from a twig, he " slicked " back into the hole as though a gigantic elastic band had drawn him from behind. In a second he reappeared, and this time emerged bodily. He was closely followed by his wife, and when her capacious person had ceased to block the entrance, out came the four cubs in a scuffle of triumphant exit.

The cubs at once made a bee-line for the nearest pine trees and began to nose about the ground at the roots. They had learnt from their parents that all manner of insects are to be found here, nestling against the bark just below the earth-line—insects which, descending the tree trunk, have crept into the crevice that always exists between the earth and the trunk of these rough-barked trees. The four made off like so many little pigs, the weakly cub accompanying his sister, who was less likely than his brothers to cuff him out of it when food was found.

In the meantime the male badger set off to-wards the open riding that bordered the warren, somewhat grumpily, and evidently with some fixed destination, while the female, after a breath of fresh air, returned underground. Presently she reappeared, pushing and hustling ahead of her

a huge bundle of dry grass, which she nosed forth
from the main entrance. Then she disappeared
for another load, and yet another, leaving each
at the mouth of the hole from which she emerged,
there to be scattered and trodden in by the
occupants of the warren. This, then, accounted
for the huge mounds of earth by some of the
burrows, for each mound, though it looked like
earth, consisted of at least ninety per cent dis-
charged bedding.

In the meantime a dispute arose amongst the
cubs as to the possession of a maimed and dis-
abled frog which had had the misfortune to leap
into their midst, and which, during the scramble,
the weakly one accidentally sat upon. Weak
though he was, he had the sense to sit still while
his brothers and sisters nosed round for the
hidden treasure, and when, somewhat crestfallen,
they relinquished the hunt, the weakly cub got
up and swallowed the frog—whole! Of course it
stuck in his gullet, and his sister—who seemed to
have an inkling as to what had happened—came
to his assistance and appeared anxious to look
down his throat, hopeful no doubt that his frantic
efforts would result in the reappearance of the
precious frog.

Having bundled from the various burrows all
the stale bedding from within, the female—or
" sow " as the keepers of the great forest vulgarly
called her—joined her cubs and seemed somewhat anxious about the weakling, who was still
gasping and coughing. She sniffed him over, then
cuffed his two brothers as being the most likely

cause of his plight. Finally she set off in the direction father had taken across the open riding, the cubs following. A motor car with gleaming headlights rattled along the Bournemouth Road only ninety yards away, but the badgers took not the least notice of it.

In the half-light in the centre of the clearing they met the old dog badger, who was hustling a tightly packed ball of grass ahead of him, half carrying, half pushing it between his chin and his forepaws, and getting very hot and irritable over the whole business. His two unruly sons seemed to regard his plight as a real bank holiday affair and gaily lent a hand, at which they were promptly cuffed out of the way. Their mother then took the bundle and proceeded back towards the earth, only the weakly cub following her, the other three, who had had enough of the earth and were out to see the world, following their father.

Just across the riding there grew a large patch of dry grass, and most of this the dog badger had torn and raked up, rolling it into compact bundles ready for transportation to the warren. So, during the early hours of this night, the male and female badgers equipped the warren with clean, dry bedding, carrying it bit by bit from the grass patch to the earth. The tiny she-cub helped a little, while the other three got in the way a good deal, and ere long the whole vicinity of the warren was littered with grass, while a distinct runway existed to and from the grass plot, indicating clearly that this was a badger warren. Once every ten days the bedding was renewed in this way—for " insectarial " reasons, as the soldier said—and once every two or three months the badgers entirely vacated the warren for some days, allowing it to air and sweeten up, so that the various epithets that reflect upon the badger's personal cleanliness are, it will be seen, lacking support in actual fact.

At the end of an hour or so the work began to slacken, and finally father settled himself down for a good old scratch, while the weakly cub sniffed in his ear. The whole badger family then set off on a voyage of discovery, not along the open riding, oh no! that is not the badger's method. Not even through the dark undergrowth, but along the bottom of one of those deep, square draining gutters that border almost every open riding of the New Forest. These gutters are about a foot in width and two feet or more in depth, and very soon becoming overgrown with herbage they are a pitfall for the unwary. The whole forest is crossed and checkered with them, a veritable labyrinth of hidden runways, so that the occupants of the badger warrens can come and go unseen, passing often within a few feet of the would-be observer.

Thus the family whose movements we are following pursued their leisurely way along the herbaceous tunnel, eating steadily as they went. Worms, beetles, centipedes, a vast assortment of winged and wriggling life, had fallen into the cutting, there to huddle behind the doubtful shelter of pebble or clod, but unerringly the badgers nosed them out, between intervals of nipping many a juicy slug from the grass above.

Once they all stopped and listened. Something was coming towards them along the cutting—something that grunted and snorted as its feet went pitter-pat. The female badger sniffed the air, then bore doggedly on, while nearer and nearer came the pitter-pat of paws. A ray of moonlight fell into the cutting just ahead, and across this silver patch something moved swiftly —not a rabbit, not a rat—and the cubs craned their necks to peer round mother. Then that something stopped dead and twitched into a ball. For a moment it remained thus, then turned and fled, fled for its life! The badgers took no notice, for they knew all about the construction of hedge-hogs, whose foolish habit of falling into these cuttings often accounted for a scarcity of insects in the locality of their imprisonment.

Fifty yards farther on the family emerged, crawled cautiously out, as they had crawled from the home burrow, and made their way to a patch of wild raspberry canes heavily laden with fruit, behind a pile of crumbling masonry which had evidently once been a cottage. Here there were other badgers, a whole family of them, busily gathering fruit, and it looked at first as though the tiny orchard would not prove large enough for the two females of the community. The trouble began by the weakly cub going to the wrong mother, whereupon he was scuffled. All ill-feeling, however, was soon swallowed up in the plenteousness of the harvest, and within two minutes the two females were searching, with their noses not an inch apart, for the same lost raspberry among the leaves.

Soon all the cubs resembled so many little barrels, and while their parents still guzzled, the two litters united for a friendly game. One of the unruly cubs mounted an ant-hill and menaced his fellows with naked fangs, at which the rest set to work to drag him down. Soon the castle became too hot for him, and another took his place, and so, among the ferns and soft decaying leaves, the game went on—a game played in silence in the darkest, loneliest place of all the woods.

Suddenly one of the adult badgers uttered a sound which was neither a grunt nor a bark, but a bit of both, and instantly every badger present " froze " where it stood. The little cub on the ant-hill flattened himself out, just where he lay, his neck to the ground, and the rest simply became little mounds of leaves.

An owl flew with a startling " kee-witt " from an oak away up the glade, then followed the tramp-tramp of footsteps. A lantern gleamed momentarily through the underbrush, and the cub on the ant-hill stared in wonder, the light reflected in his eyes. The footsteps and the light passed quite near along the riding, and once there sounded the whine of a dog, followed by the hoarse but muffled order, " Come to heel ". The earth-stopper was out!

Yes, to-morrow the hounds would meet, and to-night the keeper from Boldrewood was afield,

passing from warren to warren, and leaving each
closed behind him. He had no quarrel with the
badgers, this man who knew so well the wild life
of the great forest, but their burrows and prospect
shafts were so numerous that periodically he was
compelled to wage war with their kind, otherwise
there was no keeping pace with their digging.

The man passed by, and the badgers remained
hidden. For ten minutes none of them moved,
then simultaneously the two families rose and went
their respective ways, the family we have followed
progressing, at a business-like gait, back along the
cutting by which they had come.

Within ten minutes they were back at the
warren, but—oh horror!—as the female peered
from the ditch she saw the man with the lantern
working, spade in hand, opposite the main earth.
There was no other earth near, and as they took
in the situation one of the terriers that accompanied the man bounded up with a snarl and
made straight for the draining ditch.

Now a badger recognizes but one place of sanctuary—the earth—and when hard pressed he will
face fire and water in order to gain it. In a
moment the terrier was in their midst, closely
followed by his companion, and the badger
family made one desperate, mad stampede for
the big main earth which the keeper was in the
act of stopping.

Thus the man found himself in the very centre
of what appeared to him as a whole swarm of
badgers. He turned to face them, and in doing
so actually fell into the half-closed hole, com-

pletely sealing it. His lantern toppled over from
the brow and proceeded to diffuse more smoke
than light, and ere he could extricate himself a
badger and two terriers were on top of him,
scuffling for their lives.

With an oath the keeper freed himself from the
mêlée, and saw that his dogs had hold of one
badger which was struggling desperately to drag
them after it into the hole. A blow from his
spade finished the badger—one of the unruly
cubs—and from the corner of his eye the man
saw the remainder of the family head for a hole
he had already stopped. Thinking he had them
cornered, he hurried up, urging on his dogs, and
then this man, who had always respected the
badgers, saw something that made him respect
them even more.

A grunted signal passed between the two adults,
and the female hurried away, jostling, pushing,
herding her cubs ahead of her, but her mate
dallied behind, covering her back trail from the
terriers. They dashed up at him, and he met
them with squared front. There was a momen-
tary scuffle; the badger was forging on, keeping
up a running fight with both dogs, engaging them
fully, while always the female and her cubs were
twenty paces ahead.

The man went back for his lantern and hurried
in pursuit. In ten seconds he was in the midst
of dense timber, but he could still hear the snarling, scuffling, ghostly sounds ahead in the
shadows. He knew by the direction that the
badgers were heading for their second warren,

a kind of spare residence used alternatively with the one he had just closed, and it was over a mile distant.

The female badger reached a stream, deep and slow-running, its surface flaked with blossoms and grey with floating gossamer. At this point a dead tree lay across it, almost submerged, green and slippery with moss and weed. By this she crossed, her cubs closely following, while their father was making a noble stand among the twisted willows just up the bank.

Luck, however, was for once in the old badger's favour. The dogs were pressing him hard. It was no longer a matter of holding them back by means of a running engagement. One of the two was a Welsh terrier, quick as a weasel, while the other had a streak of bull terrier in its composition and could bite like fury. A dozen times already it had pinned Brock down and held him, while the Welshman snapped at his legs and tried to hamstring him, but Brock's terrible claws were doing their part, and his jaws had not been idle. The lips of the part-bull were already in rags, but now Brock was forced to a stand—forced to face his desperately earnest opponents at the stream margin, while in the distance he could see that lantern drawing nearer, nearer.

Then a protecting angel appeared in the very effective disguise of one of those half-wild sows that wander at large through the great reserve. She, too, had a family to protect, and she was among the bravest of all the wild denizens of the woods. With a roar she dashed in, right into the centre of the fray, scattering dogs to left and right and following up with an ugly chop of jaws.

The keeper himself hung back. He had some respect for mother pigs at night-time, and the delay enabled Brock to slip unseen to the slippery log and glide across.

At the other side he stopped. His fighting blood was up. It was for him to hold the way against all comers. His courage never wavered. No thought of personal escape seemed to enter his mind. Down among the lush green reeds he crouched, holding the bridge, the only place of open crossing, by which he could meet his foes one at a time.

The Welsh terrier located him in the twinkling of an eye. It could not see him but it knew exactly where he was—just across the stream there, in that clump of rushes, with his eyes watching and his throat to the ground.

The Welshman was wise. He knew of a crossing lower down which he could take. Not so the other terrier. He had, as I say, a streak of bull in his veins, which means that he was recklessly brave. He went right in without loss of time or argument, straight across the slippery log in a bee-line for the badger.

Brock read the terrier's character at a glance, and down went his head, down between his fore-paws, so that his bottom jaw was pressed against his chest, and only the tough muscles of his neck were exposed to the terrier's jaws. The latter dashed up and fell victim to the ruse. His strong jaws closed on the badger's neck in a worrying, scuffling grip, then quietly Brock uncurled.

His head rose up, and the terrier's throat came between his jaws. He gave one awful, tearing snatch, and the terrier fell limp. The keeper, hurrying up, one eye still on the sow, was just in time to see his dog dragged and trampled through the reeds, then to watch it drift away on the quiet stream like a poor, discarded garment.

With an oath he plunged across, waist-deep, dragging his dog from the water, but—too late. He flung his hands to his eyes in an impulsive gesture. "There goes the bravest dog I ever had," he said hoarsely.

There was a sound of scuffling near at hand; the Welsh terrier and the badger were keeping up the running fight. The man plunged after them, calling his dog by name. Then he found himself in the open, the long white highway stretching on either side, patchy with moonlight and the shadow of the pines. Two dark objects were in the centre of the road, twisting, turning, darting, rolling, sending up clouds of dust. The man staggered clumsily after them, this way and that, his spade upraised ready to strike, when there was a glare of headlights suddenly round the bend.

"Stop! For Heaven's sake——!"

There was a grinding of brakes, a shout, but the two struggling figures, locked in a death grip, surged on to meet the car. There was a crash, then silence.

A young man quietly dismounted. " I'm awfully sorry," he said quietly. " I couldn't stop sooner. They rolled under the very wheels."

The man with the spade stood by, panting, dripping water. " Have you killed them both?" he asked resignedly.

" No. Both went under the car, but I saw one come out the other side and dash into the woods."

There was no need to say more. There was no need even to look under the car. As the young man did so the keeper turned away.

" No, it wasn't your fault, sir," he said quietly, looking down at the shadow in the centre of the long, white road. " You did your best, but—it's been a black bitter night for me. Two dogs I've lost in the last five minutes—two of the bravest, pluckiest dogs I ever had."

But later that night, as he pursued his quiet way homewards through the scented, shadowy woods, the keeper smiled grimly to himself. " Grit, sheer grit!" he said aloud. " And her clear away with her cubs. Well, I'm glad the car didn't kill 'em both."

And this man, who knew the great forest better than any man alive, still had no quarrel with the badgers.

RUDDLE LUG

I

All day the warm rain had fallen incessantly, and now, with the coming of evening, a heavy warmth was in the air, refreshed by the scents of the sparkling foliage. There was no sound in all the valley, no distant barking of sheep-dogs, no crowing of moor game aloft—nothing but the drip-drip-drip of water. A diamond hung to every leaf in the forest, to every blade of grass in the open space across the ravine, yet the two half-grown leverets, deep in the grass in the centre of this open space, were dry and warm as they crouched, half dozing, waiting for their mother to come and feed them.

Out of the wood and across the cañon, stepping
daintily to dodge the wet, came an omen of good
luck, though there was not much luck about it
for smaller creatures who crossed his path. In all
respects he was a miniature tiger—this huge black
cat. He whisked his tail from side to side, tiger
fashion, as he contemplated deeds of murder.
Tiger sin gleamed from his eyes, and now and
then he uttered a faint rumbling in his throat.

A dozen times before he had passed this way
and found nothing, but to-night, perhaps, the
moist atmosphere was in his favour. Nature has
given to the young hare two wonderful protective
weapons—the first is inherited knowledge, bidding
him to lie still where his mother hides him; the
second is that at this age he has practically no
body scent, so that his foes may walk over him
in the grass, unbetrayed to their nostrils.

But the steaming heat of the evening kindled
and collected what scent there was, and two
yards from the form the feline stopped, one paw
raised, head aloft, delicately sniffing the air. He
corrected his course, slowly, in dead silence now,
and again sniffed. The young hares were deeply
hidden, there was not a blade of grass out of
place to betray their whereabouts, yet the great
cat leapt and landed to within an inch—landed
with forepaws wide apart, holding down the grass
and the leverets under it. Then down went his
evil head, nosing through the grass; the strong
muscles of his back writhed under the thick fur,
and into the air he flung one of the leverets.

A thin-edged plaintive scream went up on the

evening quietude. The cat fell upon his prize, snatched it up, and, with the leveret dangling limply from his jaws, bounded back towards the wood, bristling from end to end and rumbling like a panther.

Then something happened. A big yellow beast rounded the knoll and barred the way, a beast that stood up on its hind legs, its huge ears erect, so that it looked the size of a wolf. It was the mother of the leverets, and mothers of leverets are truly brave beasts—brave and formidable, for they fight with the super-strength of motherhood. The big cat crouched with a hissing snarl, terrible to look upon, watchful, waiting, but he did not drop the leveret. That was his challenge. He knew the ways of hares, and that he was more than a match for any hare on earth. An ordinary domestic cat would have turned and fled at the sight of that apparition rising from the grass, but he was not ordinary, neither was he domestic. He was nearly twice the weight of the average tom, and two years had elapsed since last he entered a human habitation. He was a master of woodcraft, a terrible fighting machine, a scourge upon the peaceful forest and the surrounding range. Thus he stood his ground, waiting for the hare to act and determined to hold on to what he held.

The mother hare acted. She performed a most extraordinary sky hop, and came down with both hind legs on the bristling feline's neck. " Thud " went the blow, with force sufficient to daze and stupefy even a terrier; then the cat and she rebounded, simultaneously, grappling as they rose, and as they fell apart a wisp of yellow hair floated away to cling to the grass tips.

The hare paused, goggle-eyed, watchful, and the cat remained crouched, growling horribly, his head turned as he glared at his opponent. He had let go the leveret as he fell, but now he stood with one paw on it in an attitude of defiant possession. Then, quick as light, he snatched it up, and again bounded for the wood; but the hare was after him in a trice. She caught him at the crest of the ravine, here deep and narrow, its bank an almost sheer descent of crumbling shale. She landed on top of him with all fours, kicking, tearing at his back with her strong hind legs, but in an instant the sinuous murderer was belly upwards in her grasp, and he too tore with his strong hind legs, tore at the soft parts where no hare can stand being torn. And, locked together, with a mingling of screams and snarls, they vanished over the edge, rolling, ricochetting, finally to land with a splash in the stream below and separate.

The leveret lay on the top of the bank all rolled up, his eyes glazed with terror; and the cat had no stomach for going back up that moving bank. He had got water into his ears, and that was about the only thing on earth calculated to take the fight out of him. Besides, the mother hare still barred the way; so he bounded back into the wood, hissing and spitting his chagrin.

The hare crept slowly back to the edge of the ridge and stood over her leveret. He never

moved. Patches of brown began to show on his
mother's fur. She was trembling. She nosed
him gently on to his feet. One could see his
heart beating through his coat, yet he was un-
harmed. He kicked a little, then nestled to his
mother's side, hiding his head under her flank.
She hopped towards the form, and he followed.
The second leveret, who so far had remained
motionless, came out at her summons, and she
led the two away, hopping a few times and then
pausing, and every time she paused they would
come up to hide under her.

At the other side of the field was a gate into
the road, and through it they went, across the
road, through another gate on the other side,
across a three-acre field, then on and up, among
boulders and rushes, till they gained the heather
line. It was an immense journey for the leverets,
the first they had ever made, but here, in a thick
clump of ling, was a second form, all ready for
them. In it their mother gave them their meal,
so long delayed, but it was the last she ever gave
them. She left them a little while later, tottering
and trembling as she went. Sick, dying though
she was, she did not forget to break her line of
scent every few paces by leaping aside, so that
no one could backtrack her to the lair of her
little ones.

At daybreak old James, the wheelwright, going
the round of his rabbit snares, found a dead hare
lying under a gate, and when he picked it up,
viewed its injuries, and saw that it was a mother,
he swore bitter vengeance for the ninetieth time

on the black cat that lived in the forest. He knew too well the signs of this brute to make any mistake, for had it not robbed his snares or mauled the rabbits in them times without number? In fact there were few things concerning the fauna of that mountainside James did not know.

As for the two leverets, when their mother did not come to them and hunger began to press, the one whom we came to know later as Ruddle Lug stole out of the form and began to nibble the grass; the other followed, but very soon he crept back. Though originally the stronger of the two he clearly was now sick, and as the days passed, and the two little orphans kept themselves alive by nibbling the grass surrounding their form, he gradually weakened. It was as though some dreadful disease was upon him, and finally his hind quarters became paralysed and he died. His death, like that of his mother, was upon the head of the black feline.

II

Ruddle Lug's little stomach was not designed for an undivided vegetable diet, and he too would have perished after a spell of misery had not old James one morning seen him feeding, marked him down, and caught him. Little Ruddle Lug was too weak to attempt to escape, and the old man, knowing the nature of his predicament, took the wee creature home.

That day Bessy, the wheelwright's cat, lost her

kittens by the remorseless fate which keeps a merciful check on the cat population—the sieve and bucket. Finding her nest empty, she sought far and wide, and returning at length for yet another forlorn look into the basket by the kitchen hearth, she saw a little creature there that filled her with wonder. He smelt like a kitten—for old James had rubbed the kittens against him ere he drowned them—yet clearly he was not a member of her original family. A baby he surely was, and her heart was soft with motherhood. She sniffed him over and he cuddled up to her. She repelled him scornfully, but could not find it in her heart to kill him, so she went away. Later in the day, when nature cried for relief, she went back to the basket, and this time her heart was won.

So little Ruddle Lug, deprived of his own birthright, came by the irony of fate to possess the birthright of Bessy's children; and strange it was that all Bessy's children had been large and black, for she too was given to running wild in the woods.

Ruddle Lug now grew apace, and it is to be feared he was hardly an ideal pet. Most of the day he spent hiding behind the old wheelwright's huge boots in the corner, and only at evening, when the two old people sat silently by the stove, did he venture forth to hop about the room in playful pursuit of Bessy.

The wheelwright's wife soon tired of her strange pet, and when one day he strolled from the back door and nibbled all the shoots from the border plants, old James caught the hare and took him into the shop. Here he clipped the tip from one of the animal's ears—ruddled him, as he himself described it—then toiling up the pastures he gave Ruddle Lug his liberty.

Fortunately for the hare he knew by instinct many of the tricks by which his kind have managed to survive amidst a world of foes, for from that hour onwards his life was crammed with thrilling incidents and hair-breadth escapes. He knew to backtrack and leap aside every few paces when coming down from the heather where now he made his home, to feed at evening in the rich pasture-lands below, and to lie low and say nothing when he heard the yap of a sheep-dog near; yet just as he knew the lessons of self-defence he had never been taught, so also was he prone to all the whims and ways that lay the hare at the footstool of its foes the whole world over.

Coming and going, Ruddle Lug stuck always to one pathway, trod, in fact, in his own footsteps night after night till his feeding-grounds were reached, and so wore a footpath, visible to even the unintelligent human eye. Similarly he never leapt over a wall when there was a gateway through which he could pass, and one night, as he was coming cautiously down, a shrill whistle sounded suddenly behind him, and he saw the figure of a man rise from the heather. He was truly wild now; up went his two great ears, pitter-pat went his feet on the beaten trail of his own making, and light as a thistle seed he sped for the gate at the pasture foot.

But across that gate was stretched a flimsy net, and into it Ruddle Lug ran. The soft folds drew about him, binding him helplessly in the twinkling of an eye, and a thin-edged scream went up on the night stillness.

The figure of the man loomed nearer, nearer. Two great hands spread out and clutched the hare. Yet those hands were gentle as they disengaged the binding net, and Ruddle Lug, though he did not know it, looked into the face of his old master, the benefactor of his babyhood.

" Ruddle Lug, as I thought," muttered the old man, grinning triumphantly. " I guess I've taught you a lesson, young man, you won't forget in a hurry. Now be off with you." And the hare was free.

It was generous of old James, one must admit, for hares were worth money, and old age likes its little comforts.

Did Ruddle Lug profit by his lesson? Be that as it may, never again did he run through an open gateway, and thus the menace of his human foes, of that section of them who are afield at night, was very much reduced.

Many times that autumn James saw his hare and knew him from afar, because he was the only hare that had learnt the peril of the net and lived to profit by his learning. Away little Ruddle Lug would go, as fleet now as any of his kind, presently to mount a wall, watch and listen, then bound down and on.

This manner of progressing was of advantage to the hare in yet another way, for it enabled him, while evading the net, to keep watch on any passing foe. The mounting of the wall was, indeed, exactly analogous to the sky hops of the hares of the level plains, made every few paces to see the surrounding country.

Often Ruddle Lug saw the black feline prowling back and forth from the wood, and once, meeting accidentally almost face to face, Ruddle Lug did what his mother had done, stood straight up with ears a-cock, and the cat, rumbling maliciously, turned in another direction.

Ruddle Lug was not yet in his prime, yet he was a fine sample of the brown valley hare. He had speed and wind, and experience had taught him that danger always lay ahead when one crossed the sky-line, therefore he crossed it as seldom as possible, but kept to the hollows.

One evening, when he came down from the moors, this danger was brought home to him with savage force. His face was towards the glory of the sunset, so that he could not see what lay in the shadowy hollow ahead, and topping the ridge suddenly he found himself right on top of a shepherd's portable hut, moved there during the day. The man sat at the door, smoking, at his feet his two bright-eyed, gaunt-limbed sheep-dogs. They saw the hare on the sky-line even before the man did, and were up and away in hot pursuit. Ruddle Lug, taken by surprise, unable to define his foes, dodged to left and right, then came on towards them. To have doubled back would have meant losing time, and also taking a steep downward slope on which a hare is at his worst, for it throws all his weight on his comparatively feeble forelegs. Now the dogs were taken by surprise, the hare zigzagged between them, and it was they, not he, who lost time in turning. By the time they were properly in pursuit again Ruddle Lug had dodged under the cabin at the man's very feet, shot from the other side, so that the cabin barred their vision, and was making off through the hollows, always through the hollows.

" Pitter-pat, pitter-pat," went Ruddle Lug's paws on his own beaten track, and away he sped, gliding, floating, soaring, a wonderful running machine, fooling his foes at their own splendid game.

But the luck was against Ruddle Lug that night. Over the wall he went and into the road, almost at the point at which he and his mother crossed in their one lone journey together, then off down the broad highway in a little cloud of dust. Then round a bed in the road, straight towards pursuers and pursued, there came a swift, grey automobile.

All Ruddle Lug saw was a mighty glaring light, that dazed him into terror as he ran to meet it. He peered, undecided, then, hearing the roar of machinery, he doubled back to meet his pursuers. The dogs knew what cars were and separated, one over either wall, and Ruddle Lug found himself held, the straight wide road ahead, the roar of machinery, the glaring, terrifying lights behind. Now the true hare came out in him and nearly proved his undoing. He trusted to his speed, his glorious speed, the greatest of all his gifts; he kept to the broad open way, where his speed was at its best, instead of making for shelter. And the car came on with a gathering roar, crept up to him, held him in the strong glare of its headlight, and forced him on—on, now, for the first time in his life, straining every muscle in a vain attempt to get away.

Into the leafy tunnel of the forest they went, and here the road was still wet from recent rains —wet and heavy to the feet of the hare. He put forth all his strength in a final, supreme effort, another hundred yards they went, then terror fell upon him.

" I'll have to stop," said the driver of the car. " The head-lamp is going out." He removed his foot from the accelerator, the car slackened, but Ruddle Lug sped on, gloriously triumphant at last.

" Goodness, what a chase!" muttered the motorist. He dismounted and looked at the head-lamp, then straightened himself with an exclamation, marvelling at the extraordinary powers of so small a beast. The flame of the lamp was burning as brightly as ever, but the lens was coated with dense, brown mud, flicked up by the hind legs of the hare, and not only the lens but the whole front of the car from the dumb irons to the wind-screen—dripping liquid mud!

Ruddle Lug went his way triumphant in the sense that he had surely now outdistanced and outrun the most terrible of his foes; and so he came to glory in his own powers, even to revel in a breathless chase by those whom he could foil at any time he chose. A few nights later, returning to the moor, he saw the wild cat crossing the pastures on its way back to the wood. Whether the thing he did next was planned or accidental we cannot say. We can only go by facts. He went to a ridge overlooking the shepherd's hut, and sat there, slick on the sky-line, scratching his ear. The dogs dashed out in noisy pursuit, and he led them down into the valley. On his way he all but collided with the wild cat. He stopped, ran round the bristling vision of sin, mingling his scent with that of the feline, and in a moment was lost in the gloom.

The great cat rose from the grass and met the dogs. Terrible and forbidding he stood, eyes flaming, claws exposed, but those dogs were brave. One of them dashed in and chopped. The cat dodged, a veritable pinwheel of flying claws, then—alas for him!—his nerve failed. He turned and fled, and the dogs overhauled him, threw him, chopped him, and in the silver dawn they tore him limb from limb.

III

There is something in the wild life of the hills that breeds hares of exceptional vigour, and though in Ruddle Lug there still remained the gaunt and straddle-legged effect of youth, loose-skinned and high-shouldered, there was one who knew the ways of hares who saw in him already a beast of exceptional powers. He had tried issue with every sheep-dog of note belonging to the lower range. Some were fast, others possessed wolfish staying powers, but each and every one he had set at naught. The opening fifty yards of the chase were sufficient to show Ruddle Lug with what sort of a pursuer he had to deal, and he would choose the course accordingly. Old Booth's dog was slow but deadly sure, and him Ruddle Lug would lead out on to the highway, which retained but little scent, leave him far behind, then dodge over the wall and down into the wood, while the dog blundered after the lost scent, wagging his tail in unmerited gratification.

Stephen's dog, on the other hand, was fast, and when the chase had led him to the loose rocks of the upland heights, as it always did, he invariably returned a few minutes later, limping painfully.

Thus, confident in his own powers, this creature, to whom nature had given no chosen sanctuary, moved in unfettered freedom amidst his crowded foes, their wits to his, his speed to theirs, and if he so much as failed in a single move he would pass with the thousands of his kind who fall beneath life's first and fiery test.

There came to the village three men with dogs —two such dogs as belong not to the hills. Swift and bright-eyed they were, of silken, shining coats, and their legs were like the legs of antelopes. Endlessly graceful, keen and quick-jawed, they had come in response to a challenge from the laird, who, having watched a coursing match in the eastern counties, had waxed eloquent concerning the " big light-coloured hares of our hills ".

" Brought up in rough country," he said, " pursued by every herd and stray dog, *our* brown hares know a trick or two that would set your greyhounds thinking."

The laird's nephew loved his dogs, and was confident that no hare on earth, be he of the hills or plains, could hold his own against a well-matched leash.

To-day we were to see, and old James it was who led the party, with the two greyhounds ready to be slipped, up into the coarse grass of Black Allotment. Up started a hare, away with ears a-cock, sliding silently through the rushes, and the noble dogs, straining at their leash, were slipped. Old James looked at the laird and winked. " That's him," he muttered, and the laird there and then made a bet with his nephew that the hare would get away—no conditions, simply that the hare would get away. Old James winked again, for he had seen the ruddled ear.

Watching behind him, Ruddle Lug set the pace easily, breasting the slope. Then ere he could realize it, his pursuers were upon him, one at either side, ranging wide, but slowly drawing in. He was startled, horrified by their speed. Never before had he met the equal to it. He turned in his own length, dodged under the buttocks of the nearer hound, leaving the other far behind, then, as they checked their headlong plunge, Ruddle Lug was up and over the crumbling wall.

Both hounds came on with scarcely a second

lost. The first cleared the wall with a foot to
spare, the second landed heavily, but the rumble
of masonry that followed found him yards away.
Up went their ears, brightly shone their eyes, as
they sought for the hare. Out in the open they
looked, but there was Ruddle Lug, speeding for
his life, *under* the wall towards the heights. The
field cheered his prowess, but one of the hounds
saw him and on they went, nearly a mile at
breathless speed up the steep mountainside. Near
to the high boundary wall Ruddle Lug was turned.
He had made a desperate bid to gain the heather,
but to attempt that ten-foot leap of the boundary
wall, with his pursuers at his heels, would have
been madness. He doubled back, in among the
boulders and the rushes; and the nephew said:
" Your hare is lost."

Old James smiled grimly. " Not yet," was all
he answered. One dog was between the hare
and the heather, heading him off from the only
safety he knew, and there among the boulders,
among the tangled rushes, Ruddle Lug flashed
in and out, twisting, turning, doubling back. Here
the speed of his foes was set at naught; it was a
hindrance to them, for they used up their energy
checking futile dashes, recovering, dashing again,
while Ruddle Lug twisted and dodged with ease.
The greyhounds' tongues were lolling; they were
unused to such country, unversed in such tactics;
and when the coming of the men forced Ruddle
Lug to face the perilous downward grade, he did
so with a start of forty yards and with the speed
of his pursuers culled of its keenest edge. A mile

from the spectators the hounds turned him, but among the rank thistles he got away again, then on towards the burn, towards the village, and, at last, through a gate.

Old James looked at the laird. "He's hard pressed," said the wheelwright, and the laird nodded. The bet hung in the balance.

But the bars of that gate were narrow, and while Ruddle Lug slipped through easily, the hounds collided heavily with the bars, and one of them whimpered with pain. Priceless seconds were lost ere they thought to leap the wall, and Ruddle Lug was half across that dreaded stretch of open pasture they had forced him to take. But the hounds reduced that distance to a third, and at the burn Ruddle Lug was again in mortal peril.

He knew the crossing well—had used it more than once to foil a swift pursuer—a pointed, slippery boulder in midstream, twelve feet from either bank. Pitter-pat went his paws, thump-thump went his heart against his lean ribs. He leapt and landed, seeming scarcely to touch, and floated on, away up the green bank behind Stephen's outhouses. The hounds too leapt, from different points but simultaneously, and both for the self-same boulder. They met in mid-air and crashed apart into the shallow water of the burn, and the field, coming on, saw the hare gliding away—forty, fifty, sixty yards of start.

"My word, *some* hare!" cried the nephew. "They'll lose him among the farm buildings." And he held out his hand to shake with the laird.

The farm buildings were a place of many obstacles and mingled scents, and there Ruddle Lug had fooled many a persistent pursuer. To-day scent was no factor, wits and speed alone could count, and now, as he set his weary limbs to enter, there rushed along the narrow way to meet him the only dog who knew his tricks and had speed enough to profit by his knowledge— Stephen's dog!

Ruddle Lug would easily have fooled him singly, but now he was turned back to meet his old pursuers, forced to take the only open way, which now they held. He had run six miles at breathless speed, and here, at the back of the village, men and boys began to appear at every gate, all eager to help the dogs but with little enough pity for the hare. Straight towards the greyhounds he went, in and out between them, then straight for the only way of exit—a stile on the stone wall. On one side was the burn, on the other a group of men, behind him the dogs, and ahead the village, so he made for the village. Through the stile, across the cobbled yard, through yet another gate, and on to the broad highway. Down the main street he headed, with dreaded humans everywhere, and a little cloud of dust hid his going. Another dog dashed out, cut him off, turned him back, but he doubled again and faced this dog when he saw the grey-hounds so close—dodged it and was through.

Straight ahead was the open road, on the left lay the river, brown and swollen by recent rains, on the right a row of cottages, and behind a

motley throng of men and dogs with the greyhounds leading. Faster and faster still sped
Ruddle Lug, his face again toward his beloved
hills, when on the white highway ahead he saw
men, many of them, running to meet him. It
was the field, caught up at last, and now they
barred the way, cut off his one retreat.

The heart of Ruddle Lug failed at last. How
could he live, a solitary little creature with all the
world against him, and only his speed to see him
through? Hard pressed by the hounds, he
doubled to the left, but here the river cut him
off. To the left again, back along its bank, but
here Stephen's dog was speeding to meet him,
and behind the dog were many boys and men.

Then Ruddle Lug made his choice. If he were
to die, could he not do it triumphant to the end?
They saw him turn and leap high and far. Far
out over those angry waters he leapt, to be caught
by the smother of foam and borne away.

The nephew hung his head. He had lost his
bet, but that he did not mind. Was this the
crowning glory of the chase? He had seen his
dogs fooled, saw them now searching for the hare
that fooled them, but not that alone had touched
his manhood. He had seen a wonderful little
creature, hard pressed by man and dogs, leap
recklessly to its death, game to the end, choosing
its own fate when the moment came, and choosing
it triumphantly.

Then the cry went up—" The hare! The
hare!" They saw him washed ashore, saw him
scrambling up the sandy bank, blindly, gasping

9

for life, and the greyhounds also saw. Straight
and true they dashed to meet him, yet he never
stirred. They were upon him now, and a woman
covered her eyes with a cry of pity. Then the
hare leapt, and the hounds passed under him.
One of them lost its footing on the sandy bank
and a second later was swept away. The other
recovered and renewed the chase, joined by
Stephen's dog.

Slowly now went Ruddle Lug, his dash and
glory gone. The water filled his coat and weighed
him down—blind, dazed, half-drowned, he had
no fight left. Yet before him stretched the white
highway, and beyond that his beloved hills. It
was a straight run back to life and freedom, but
his strength was gone.

At the tiny bridge the dogs were all but upon
him, when suddenly the hare's strength came
back in a final desperate burst of speed. He held
his own for forty yards, and there, at the bend
in the road, suddenly there swung into view a
large, grey automobile. There was a shout, a
squeaking of brakes, but—too late. Little Ruddle
Lug passed under the car, under that torturing
roar of machinery, but the dogs were larger than
he. There was a crash, a yelp, and there in
respective gutters lay two good dogs, struggling
to rise from the dust into which they were beaten.

Slowly, painfully, towards the unending heather
line, Ruddle Lug made his way—risen supreme
above his foes, gloriously triumphant, the hour
of his life's crowning peril safely passed.

DRIFTS OF WINTER

I. THE HARVEST MOON

It was the Indian summer—that magic season
of the year. The first frost had stayed the flow
of sap in the alders and willows that lined the
river, and the leaves were drifting to the earth in
gold and crimson showers. The days were breathlessly still; the silver strands of gossamer floated
motionless in the shafts of light that fell across
the stream; and the sweet, fresh scent of the spray
hung everywhere. The nights were dark and
silent, wreathing the lower hollows in fairy cloud-
banks, eerily beautiful under the stars.

On either side the woods were astir with furtive, scurrying life—a thousand little woodland

denizens garnering the harvest against the weeks of cold and hunger drawing near, and Starprint, the water-vole, was to some extent affected by the bustle and stir. He nibbled and searched from dawn to dusk, in and out of the water, daintily stripping the seeds of their husks with his delicate forepaws, and so laying on fat which would help him to contend with the days of cold and hunger ahead; he too was garnering the harvest.

At night-time Starprint often swam the river and ventured high into the wood above the fairy mist wraiths, returning with the root of a wild hyacinth stolen from the perilous, whispering world without. He went in mortal terror, for the water-vole knew but one friend, recognized but one place of sanctuary—the river. Away up in the wood the falling of a leaf sent him quivering among the ferns, and such was the desperation of his fear, away from his beloved element, that, meeting a grey-eyed old angler one dusk, he sat in the centre of the path, shivering with terror and gnashing his chisel teeth in wild defiance.

Since their coming of age last summer Starprint and his brothers and sisters had, like wise relatives, lived their solitary little lives apart, meeting often on the mossy stones to nibble each other's faces in friendly greeting, then going each its respective way to a home it shared with no one. Starprint had no experience to teach him of the lean months ahead, yet the roots and fungi retrieved from his perilous nightly raids he carefully hoarded in a shallow emergency burrow he

had engineered among the roots of a fallen plane,
fully a dozen yards from the water's edge.

The emergency burrow was merely a store-
room, for all summer the vole had lived and had
his being among the corridors of the loose rocks
that lay in a chaos of disorder along the water's
edge, and as the Indian summer lingered on, his
store was completed. With time to idle now, he
would sit on a mossy stone far out in the river,
watching the darting dippers, and singing at intervals a strange little squeaking song like no other
sound on earth. All Nature seemed at peace with
herself during this time of plenty—old feuds were
laid aside and old wrongs forgotten.

Starprint would calmly sit, watching with his
bright black eyes, while the grey-eyed old angler
waded by within a yard or two, and so the water-
vole came to know not only the angler but also
the kingly fish the man pursued. They came
from the sea, crowding every pool and hover, and
each and every one was bent on its uphill voyage
—on and up, in a vague, unending quest; and
often, while Starprint sat and sang, a silver king
would rise from the water quite near to him,
slashing upwards in a thousand rainbow flashes,
to sink back with a splash that shook the very
river bed. But Starprint was not afraid of the
salmon, and similarly, in the plenteousness of the
Harvest Moon, he had forgotten his terror of
Mawakee, the otter, and of Quask, the keen-
eyed heron.

Then one night the wind began to blow. The
leaves whirled everywhere, and it was as though

the ghost armies of winter were holding council in every shadowy nook. A lapwing, borne helplessly on the wings of the gale, was dashed into the trees, and fell dead at the water's edge.

With the dawning of winter, Starprint's infant fears returned. The mad whirl of the leaves suggested the swoop of the death-dealing owl, a branch falling in the river rekindled his infant dread of Mawakee, and instinctively Starprint knew that to-night opened a new era in his life.

II. THE HUNGER MOON

The wind ceased; the rain began to fall with a thunderous hiss. It filled the rugged watercourses away up in the hills, and before daybreak Starprint was flooded out from his home among the rocks.

Whether or not the water-vole had any preconception of this inevitable catastrophe when he set to work and made his spare burrow, digging it high above the highest water-line, we cannot, of course, decide; but to the spare burrow he now went, apprehensive of the sullen change the last few hours had wrought in the world about. Here he could afford to laugh at the storm, for a cosy bedroom, lined with moss, awaited him, while in an adjoining chamber was his plenteous winter store.

Next day the wind veered to the north, the rain changed to snow, and the water-vole was buried in. He belonged now to that vast underworld which, while the Snow King reigns, claims a kindred of its own, a world of sleeping life, unseen, unsought, secure beneath winter's kindly mantle; and while the gaunt-limbed spectres of death searched the solitude without, Starprint, like a million million of his race, slept in plenteous security.

But, as the Harvest Moon had lingered, so now the Hunger Moon outstayed its welcome, and Nature, playing her cards impartially, one day sent the leanest and craftiest of all those spectres of hunger to Starprint's home. The warmth of the little vole's body had thawed away the snow about the entrance of the burrow, and into the black recess the red fox poked his lean and hungry nose. He filled his gaunt body with one long draught, exhaled with a force which, had there been a back way, would assuredly have blown the vole out of it; then, arching his long tail, he began to scratch.

Behold now the wisdom of Starprint's guardian instincts. Nature had whispered to him to lay aside a winter store, to hide it high above the highest water-line, and to make there for himself a cosy bed. He might have chosen the sandy bank for this retreat, but again the guiding voice had whispered: " No! Hide your store deep among the roots, where no creature larger than yourself can scratch you out." So among the roots Starprint had made his winter home, and now, as the fox scratched savagely at the entrance, the little vole, desperate with terror, extended his narrow shaft in and out among the twisted roots, so that, had Reynard known it, each minute found him farther from the realization of his quest. He reached the storeroom and scattered wide its contents, he littered Starprint's bed upon the trampled snow, then with a snarl of defeat he vanished ghost-like into the world of ghosts.

Just before dawn the vole crept cautiously forth to survey the havoc of his home. An awful fear of the place was upon him, and the old dumb bidding to put running water between himself and the place of peril. The scent of the fox was every-where, yet between here and the river lay thirty feet of unbroken white expanse.

Starprint summed up his courage and made a dash for it; but as his feet sank in the snow a ghastly, deathly scream, that froze the very blood in his veins, sounded from an alder near. Down came the white-and-yellow owl, toppling through the gloom on silent wings; but she was half a second too late, and half a second in the wild makes a world of difference. Starprint struggled weakly on and slithered down the icy bank to meet the water with a flop, while the owl came tobogganing in pursuit at his very heels, its wicked claws gashing deep furrows in the snow.

Starprint's confidence returned as he felt again the friendly water, and with a sense of triumph he set off along the river bed, running in and out among the stones, and heading—oh foolish step!—for the opposite bank. Midway across his lungs gave out and he was compelled to rise, while the owl was waiting for him. He dived instantly as she struck, but progressing slowly now, scarcely six inches below the surface, it

AT HIS VERY HEELS

seemed his fate was inevitably sealed. His lungs
were bursting, he was becoming paralysed with
fear, while just overhead, on winnowing wings,
screaming horribly and staring down at him with
great bewitching eyes, waited the owl.

Two feet more, then—down the great bird
came, striking the water with a splash. Her big,
hooked talons cleaved the rippling surface, and
Starprint, with the same terrified bravery that
had possessed him when one purple autumn dusk
he had faced the angler, seized a crooked claw
with his chisel teeth—clutched and held till his
fangs grated against the bone.

One awful scream of rage rang across the phosphorescent quietude, and Starprint was hurled
a dozen paces, spinning grotesquely through the
air, while the great owl struck and slashed at
him as he fell. But luck was with the vole
that night, as indeed she always is with those
of his kind who live to see the spring. The owl
had tossed him in the direction he wished to go,
and he met the water with a flop just where a
broken wooden fence jutted out from the bank,
its bars festooned with a trailing drapery of drift-
weed. Under this sheltering mass Starprint lay,
holding with his forepaws, his body swaying idly
with the tide; and there he remained, a part of
his surroundings, while the owl sat on the rail-
head not a yard away and tucked each feather
into place, grumbling savagely at her defeat.

High in the wood was a small round crystal
pool, overshadowed with pine and briar, a place
of fairy loveliness in its wintery dell, and here Star-

print now made his home. In the bank of the pool he found the summer dwelling of a hateful grey rat, but the owner had gone back to the sewers and pigsties for the winter months, and promptly Starprint set to work to adapt the residence to his own requirements. His first act was to dig an emergency exit which tapped the pool well below the water-line, so that he could come and go unseen, and emerging from the pool bed in the shallow water his moving paws stirred up a cloud of mud which hid him as he ran, thus answering the same purpose as does the ink fluid of the cuttlefish. Yet another cunning thing he did, which at first puzzled the grey-eyed angler when next he visited the pool. An oak bough had fallen and splintered into fragments on the bank of the pool, and one of the logs had rebounded into the water. Starprint swam with the log into the centre of the pool, and there he anchored it with a rush, so that it could move a little in the breeze.

The Frost King came again and the pool was quickly frozen over, save for a circular space about the drifting log. Thus Starprint, emerging by his under-water shaft, could prospect for food about the bed of the pool, rising for air and perhaps to sit and sun himself at his floating raft.

Nor was it long ere the real value of this wise provision came to light, for one night Mawakee, the otter, came up to the pool in the heart of the wood. She glided over the drifts and stood on the snowy bank, with her wonderful head uplifted, an endlessly graceful creature in the silver gloom; then she slid down the bank and out on to the ice.

She found Starprint's burrow and tore it up with claws and fangs. Starprint fled by the under-water exit and lay beneath his raft, watching her, only the tip of his nose visible, impervious to the cold, for under his ample coat was the thick layer of fat laid on during plenteous autumn days.

Next Mawakee found the raft, then Starprint fled to what remained of his shaft, and at its broken mouth, away up on the bank, filled his lungs. Back and forth the otter hunted him a dozen times, but always he was gone a second before she arrived, so in the end she gave it up.

Where now should Starprint go? Twice his home had been broken up during that reign of terror, and thrice his guardian angel had piloted him through hours of deadly peril. No longer could he regard the pond as a place of sanctuary, and so he turned again to his old, old friend, the only friend he knew on earth—the river.

III. THE HONEYMOON

Back to the boulder labyrinth of those sunny autumn days—and yet, how things were changed! Where were his brothers and sisters? Had the merciless weeding out of winter claimed them all?

There followed days of driving mist and drenching cloud wraiths—short days and long nights, with death and hunger prowling as playmates. Starprint lived a solitary, watchful life, till one

evening, when the clouds momentarily cleared
and the river shone like burnished copper, he
heard a splashing, familiar sound that called him
forth from his cranny.

There, at the shallow margin of the pool,
diving, landing, diving, clearly enjoying herself
immensely, he found a little lady vole whose coat
was of a russet hue. Whence she had come he
did not know, but evidently she was of the fittest
of her kind, for she too had survived the pitiless
weeding out of the Hunger Moon. She looked
at him with her little black, lachrymose eyes,
while the spray hung on her coat in a thousand
scintillating diamonds. Starprint swam up to her,
and side by side they sat on the mossy stone, and
exchanged their friendly greeting, and when the
she-vole dived again Starprint followed.

Many things have changed since the waning
of the Harvest Moon. Mawakee, the beautiful,
had become a prowling terror; Quask, the keen-
eyed heron, was a lightning-dealing peril to anything he fancied he could swallow; and even the
silver kings of the pool had become black and ugly
—ugly in looks as in disposition. Two of the
mighty fish had taken possession of the pool where
Starprint and his friend were swimming, and now
the male fish, sabre-toothed and hook-jawed, was
savagely fighting his way towards the stone to
which the two voles had returned.

He came like a wave of fire, the water surging
from his ruddy flanks, and rearing his ugly head
above the surface he snatched the she-vole from
the stone and bore her under.

In an instant Starprint's fighting blood was up. Once, in bygone days, he had seen his sister dragged under by a giant trout; he had watched two of his brothers done to death by a polecat; and as each time he fled in terror from the place, no thought had occurred to him save for his own precious safety. Not so to-day. Something terrible and new throbbed through every fibre of his tiny being, and, as he saw the she-vole borne away between those rending, crocodile jaws, he hurled himself to her defence with never a thought for his own great peril.

Starprint rushed at the mighty fish and alighted upon its head—hanging on with his small, sharp claws, getting his chisel teeth to work in deadly earnest. In an instant he was flung a yard or more amidst a smother of foam. A roar of water filled the air, then Starprint and his friend broke surface, swimming side by side for the friendly rock, while in the opposite direction surged the mighty fish, leaving a thin train of crimson to mingle with the foam as he returned to his redd.

Side by side they sat in the soft winter glow. The fire-play around them was touched with fairy tints. The wonderful mosses on the rocks shone out amidst the gloom in brightest, loveliest shades. High in the wood a ring-dove " cooed " as though to remind the weary, watchful world that spring was surely somewhere near. Starprint helped to lick the she-vole's little hands with his warm soft tongue, then they swam off together through the light and purity of that dawning world of theirs.

A wonderful world indeed—dawning clean and

new, with every hour, for a million million of God's gentle children. We ourselves grow old; but if the sunlight loses its magic, if the romance and beauty fade from the voice of the wind that bears the drifting leaves to earth, if the coming and going of the seasons merely marks for us the sorrowful passage of time by which all lives are numbered, then we ourselves are the only old and tarnished things in a world for ever wonderful and new.

Spring came at last, and down there by the pool foot, where the sunlight fell in slanting shafts through the forest spires, where Mawakee had her home and moved at peace with the happy kindred all around, the sand was dotted and laced with countless star-like prints—the tracks of Starprint and his children.

THE GENTLEMAN HOBO

I

He was the ugliest dog that the blood and
ingenuity of the canine race could bring into
being. Part bull-dog he was, or rather his head
was bull-dog unadulterated, but his tail was
whippet, his legs were spaniel, and his body
savoured of Dalmatian hound. Imagine, if you
can, what that means; add to it white, wall eyes,
the coat of a mottled Dane, and a soul of gold—
of purest, cleanest gold. No, I cannot describe
Hobo, so picture him as you will, the type of
pup which, by the principles of humanity, should
be drowned at birth, because the world is a cruel
place and has no vacancy for such ugliness.

How Hobo came to live in the North End
Park, many who saw him wondered. It was a
large park—a picturesque wilderness of oak and
beech laid off for the public on the precincts of

the city. The recent exhibition had occupied but the merest corner of it, and Hobo's master was one of the men employed in putting together the temporary exhibition stalls. Hobo and he had " camped out " all spring under the pavilion by the baseball ground; they had seen the show through, then had dallied with several others in order to remove and cart away the buildings.

It was during this closing performance that one day they took Hobo's master to hospital on a handcart. He had been ill several days, and finally he fell off a roof—fainted, I suppose. His mates shook their heads gravely, spoke of double pneumonia and concussion on top of it, but all that Hobo knew was that his master had vanished into thin air.

The boy's mates fed Hobo while they were there—that is, when he would take food from them, which was not often. Hobo was searching for someone, you see, someone he could not find. He spent his days running from workman to workman, looking up wistfully into their faces, till the words: " No, I ain't him, old son!" grew sad by iteration. It never occurred to Hobo to search beyond the park, for here he and his master had spent their lives since that distant day when as stowaways they travelled south from their far-off northern woods.

In the meantime the boy with a broken head and double pneumonia, lying delirious in Ward 27, called hoarsely to his nurse every twenty minutes through the night and entreated her to feed Hobo before she went to bed. Of course she

did it immediately, or told him so—one of those
white lies which are more precious than black
pearls.

The dog's hopes fell with the falling of the
buildings, followed by the final departure of
the men. The grass sprang up again over the
trampled earth, warmed and encouraged by the
lingering " Indian Summer ", and to this sacred
area Hobo at first confined himself.

Very soon a new factor began to come into
play—hunger. Had Hobo been a city-bred dog
he might have flourished exceedingly by the ex-
ploration of garbage heaps; but he was schooled
in the woods, and the purity of that land
where he had spent his puppy days influenced his
movements throughout. He was a curious dog
in many respects, in so far as all bull-dogs are
curious, and since his head was bull-dog we can
conclude that his brain was bull-dog too. Anyway, he was bull-dog by temperament, bull-dog
to the core.

Just as there are human beings who readily
adapt themselves to their environment, be it for
good or ill, so there are dogs. There are men
and dogs who will starve in the midst of plenty,
just because their sense of honour, or propriety,
or pig-headed conservatism—call it what you will
—presents a closed gate to them, while there are
others who will immediately adapt their habits to
their habitat, acquiring methods which, though
easily taken up, are not so easily abandoned
when circumstances change again. It is thus, by
a day's misfortune, that the taint of the scavenger

or the thief may fall upon a dog's name, though he be of spotless ancestry.

Hobo had lived clean, and that bull-dog brain of his rendered it impossible for him immediately to adapt himself to the new order. For a time he went hungry, very hungry; because the emptiness at his heart swallowed up the emptiness of hunger; but one sunny morning, when the squirrels were in the leaves and the gossamer floated on the still air, he heard voices floating up from a hollow near, the voices of children. The sound appealed to his sense of loneliness, and he raced in its direction—his wall eyes gleaming hungrily, saliva dripping from his massive jaws.

Rabies had not been unknown during the summer months, and every child of the district had been solemnly warned by its parents against the peril of the dog that " runs straight ". So, when the little band of explorers saw that awful apparition bearing down upon them, they scuttled for cover with screams of " mad dog!" They scuttled—all but the baby, who sat on a sun-baked mound, conspicuous in a crimson woolly jacket, cooing to the sunshine and the flowers and to all the opening joy of life, and there was no fear at his heart as the awful creature bounded up—simply because, to him, the world contained no ugliness.

Hobo licked the little fellow's face, fawned over him caressingly, and finally took the wet, warm biscuit proffered—quite accidentally—in pink, soft fingers. Then the baby yelled, which

stirred the hero spirit in the leader of the band,
himself still the possessor of milk teeth. Boldly
he came forth from his hiding, that little nine-
year-old, and used his feet with desperate spirit
on Hobo's bony flanks. " How dare you bite
our baby!" he cried; but Hobo had felt caresses
a good deal heavier, and as their eyes met the
colour came back to the little hero's cheeks.
" Say," he cried to his band of vanquished
followers, " he ain't mad at all! He's the dearest
old dog in all the park!"

Hobo spent the day with the little holiday-
makers, shared their lunch of bread and pumpkin
tart out of a cheap red hamper, and finally wound
up the delightful experience by a thrilling squirrel
hunt at the north end of the park, still fragrant
with faded flowers. But at dusk Hobo went
his way, and they went theirs—looking wistfully
back at each other till the gathering gloom intervened.

Next day the lonely dog was back in the
hollow glade, looking for his playmates. He found
them not, but he found other children, and they
too greeted him with the touch of happiness and
friendship. Thus Hobo learned what many of us
cannot or will not learn, that all children are the
same, be they the sons of Dukes or of Cobblers.
So in due course he became known to hundreds
of children as the North Park Dog, the dog
which loved all children, the dog which was
always searching, looking for someone, but refused more than a passing handshake with any
adult human—above all, the dog who was so

ugly that no adult human was likely to court
more than his passing fellowship. Thus many a
dog who, through lack of breeding or misfortune
of circumstance, becomes a pariah, counts among
his friends only the little people of the parks and
alleyways, and, robbed of all other sympathy,
turns to them for the caresses that his ancestry
with man make necessary to his existence.

As to how Hobo was subsisting all this time—
that first day with the squirrels had given him a
hint. There were many squirrels at the north
end of the park, the large black variety in addition
to the red, and at this season all were busy cutting
down the nuts and berries and garnering them
from the leaves. So Hobo set out one dawn towards the north end. Very different now were
his tactics, for he was out for food, not to provoke
the laughter of a merry little band of followers.
There is nothing like hunger to waken the skill
of the hunter, and Hobo stole like a shadow from
tree to tree, watching, listening, till eventually he
saw two squirrels on the ground nearly half a
mile away. Slowly he stole up, keeping the tree
trunks between him and them, till finally he
darted like a whirlwind from behind the very
tree to which the squirrels belonged. One of the
two entirely lost its head, and very good eating
it proved!

Dawn and dusk, when the great park was
deserted, were Hobo's hunting hours, and every
day added something to the sum of his knowledge.
There were lean days and good days, and very
soon he acquired the habit of burying such food

as he did not immediately require near to his bed under the pavilion.

But the winds were becoming cold now, and Hobo, though he scratched up a barrier of earth round his bed, began to shiver in his sleep. Also there were wet days, when no squirrels were to be seen, and when the picnicking children, whose food he so often shared, were conspicuous by their absence. Frost followed, and Hobo's right forepaw swelled up, while the drinking-place froze over. It was also very noticeable that the squirrels were becoming fewer and fewer with the drifting of the leaves, while the few children who visited the park brought no food hampers and did not understand when he looked at them so pleadingly.

Hunger, at length, drove Hobo from the park, and for some strange reason he turned his steps northwards. Whither he was going he did not know, but in that direction, somewhere, somehow, was the thing his being craved. And on the very day of his going a pale-faced boy, hobbling between two sticks, a boy who had broken hospital bounds, sought the park from end to end, calling Hobo by name!

II

Hobo's forepaw, caught by the first frost, was almost healed now, and at a steady lope he left behind him the metalled roads. Sweeping hillsides rose in view, clothed with cedar and poplar; such woods as seemed familiar to him, for they had risen phantom-like in his dreams when he stirred and whined in his bed under the pavilion; but here there was no life, nothing but the vastness and the silence.

Now and then he passed through tiny settlements and heard mice squeaking under the raised sidewalks, and once a woman threw some hot potatoes to him. To him or at him, it did not matter much, for Hobo wolfed the potatoes and went his way refreshed—still on his vague quest for that far-off Island of Promise, still shunning garbage heaps as unclean though savoury things.

Soon the last road petered out; there was nothing left but the eternal forests. Somewhere across the radiance a lynx screamed, then a ghost fled across the whiteness ahead of Hobo—a white ghost, small and low on the ground like a patch of drifting vapour. Hobo stared, then ambled up to sniff its tracks with the steady, self-confident tread of the British bull-dog. The scent told him that the creature was good to eat, but he was new to scent-running, and in his eagerness he followed the line backwards. He followed it into a cedar clump, when from the gloom ahead there rang again that devilish snarl of temper, and Hobo saw the lynx—the lynx that had sworn because she had missed the rabbit—glaring at him from the thicket of a windfall, her tasselled ears laid back, her stump of a tail vibrating spasmodically. Hobo withdrew with a rumbling growl—not because he was afraid, for fear was unknown to him, but because he was too British to pick a quarrel with a formidable foe just for the sake of the thing. Moreover, he possessed a

British sense of ownership: this was the lynx's range, not his.

But this much was safely pigeon-holed in Hobo's mind—those grey ghosts were good to eat because they smelt good, and because the she-devil hunted them. Thereafter Hobo hunted the grey ghosts, and there were many of them. He learned immediately that they were swifter than he, and that it was no use pursuing them. His experience with the tree-dwellers now stood him in good stead, for as he had begun to hunt by strategy, so now he carried the same measures into effect. He slew his first Snowshoe by extending a sap through the snow across the open towards it, then bounding out when the rabbit's back was turned; and that night, his wild instincts properly awakened, he hollowed out a wolfish bed under the snow, and for the first night for many weeks slept happily and warmly.

There were other things to hunt in this wilderness. One evening two spruce partridges came planing over the tree tops and dived head foremost into the deep snow-drift, close to where Hobo stood. He waited for them to fall asleep, and while he waited a blinding blizzard swept up, and under cover of it Hobo slew the two birds and finally made his bed where they had hidden.

The prevailing wind was from the north, and Hobo, following the hunter's instincts as from the first, continued steadily to voyage against it. All went well with him, but oh, the utter loneliness of this land! Many days had passed since last

he saw the signs of human habitation, and he
longed for the sound of human voices and the
touch of human fingers. Here there were many
tracks in the snow; some awoke the hunter lust
within him while others spoke vaguely of danger.
He was subtly aware of this danger, for this he
knew, as many a man comes to know it, that
peril rose not from those more formidable than
himself, but from his *own kind*. There were wild
dogs in those woods, and between the wild and
the tame there lies a no-man's-land which only
a traitor can cross. Many have tried to cross that
no-man's-land, but few have lived to tell of their
crossing.

Hobo, the unchangeable, had no idea of crossing. He was still searching in his purblind,
obstinate, pig-headed bull-dog way for one whom
he had lost, irredeemably lost, and for whom any
dog but Hobo would long since have ceased to
search. He knew that he moved in hourly peril
of his life; the peril in the material form was yet
to take definite shape.

One night Hobo came to know. He was
plodding wearily over the drifts, when through
the phosphorescent whiteness ahead there appeared a great grey form, a lovely stag careering
faster than the wind, its spreading antlers sil-
houetted against the orange sky. It seemed
merely to tap the icy crests with its delicate hoofs,
and Hobo, the hunter lust awakened, would have
given chase but for something—a calm, soft voice
in the quietude which warned him not to follow.
He watched with shining eyes, then there broke

across the quietude a sound—a thin, sad, wavering sound, at first almost musical, but soaring
upwards, till a sinister note rang in its melody,
finally to cease with a series of wholly devilish
yaps. It was the blood song of the timber
wolves !

Then Hobo saw the wolves. Full into the starlight they came, five of them, not twenty paces
from him, great bristling timber wolves, green-
eyed and gaping. For an instant the bull-dog
rose up in Hobo's veins, and he would have dashed
out and chopped them, but the bull-dog was
swallowed by the yaller dog, and he crouched
lower in the drift.

When the wolves were gone, Hobo rose rapidly,
taking such a direction that the wind blew his
body scent away from the wolves, till at a distant
point it occurred to him to back-track them. He
took up their trail and followed it till it led him
out into a small frozen lake, and in the centre of
that lake lay a deer, freshly killed by the wolves,
killed, but not touched, because there was still
more killing to be done. Thus Hobo learned
what the truly wild folk of the forest always
know, that when game is abundant it is worth
while to back-track the hunting wolves.

Thus, by a ponderous analysis of his surroundings, Hobo survived where many would have
perished. Each evening he watched the tree tops
for the partridges going to roost, and when the
moon rose he would stand in the quietude listening for the wolf pack as it drifted through the
night. Always, now, before entering an open

space, he peered cautiously round the fringe, timber-wolf fashion, to see what lay ahead.

At length the game belt was left behind, the timber became small and very soon ceased entirely, but still that vague quest, that restless yearning within him, beckoned Hobo on. There was nothing now but the rolling whiteness, fairy ridges stretching in fantastic array to the sky-line. Sometimes the fireplay fell upon these ridges, streaming over their crests in cascades of shining blood, filling the hollows with a vapour of transparent gold; sometimes the footlights shifted and all things became purple, the snow, the sky, the distant buttes. At other times there was nothing but the ghostly radiance of the snow, no colour, no sound, save when the aurora rustled its silken banners, or seemed veritably to strike the buttes with its descending rockets.

So, into the barren lands, into the lands of half-light, into the lands God gave to Cain, Hobo voyaged. There were birds here, many birds, the small barren-lands ptarmigan, but always they saw him coming, and hunger befell Hobo, real hunger now, striking chill through every fibre of his body, till he became too hungry to sleep, too tired to voyage on. Sometimes the frozen crust gave way beneath his paws and he sank hopelessly, struggling and panting for an hour or more ere he could free himself from the drifts. His strength was slowly, surely giving out, but his heart, his spirit, remained unbroken. Other dogs, stronger dogs than he, would have lost courage and perished in the drifts, but Hobo had no thought of giving in. He would lie down, red-eyed and panting, watching the flocks of ptarmigan going to roost, watching with hopeful, hungry gaze, still building on catching one of them, though it was manifestly proved that such was beyond his power.

So Hobo reached the limits of his endurance and tottered over the edge. He tried to rise, panting and whining, but at length he lay on his side, stretched out, nursing what remained of his strength, the huge red sun dipping below the sky-line rimming all things with a braid of burnished gold. It trailed its fiery fingers across the snow, touching even Hobo, the ugliest of all ugly dogs, till even he was beautiful; and there his story might have finished, one of the million million unknown tragedies, call them romances if you will, that the turning of a card, the raising of a glass, the sidelong glance of a woman, may bring about—the tale of a dog who has lost his master.

Night came and Hobo slept. He was awakened by a hot scent in his nostrils, by a faint clicking sound, filling the wastes around him, by a trampling in the snow on every side, by a grunting, grunting, grunting everywhere. He rose stiffly to see a great grey shape moving by, then another and another, till the whole ghostly realm, pale under the rays of the aurora, became peopled with ghosts before his vision, all voyaging eastwards—the drifting of the caribou thousands.

Hobo struggled up. Here was life, life radiant and immense. His strength came surging back, he tottered where he stood and watched the world-old army drifting by—tens of thousands of caribou, covering the whole face of the barrens, looking as though they had voyaged thus since time began, for they were bearded and ice-crystalled like creatures of another world. Then Hobo launched himself forward, hurled himself with his last remaining strength at the foremost ghost, a yearling calf as luck would have it. Hobo obtained the bull-dog grip and five minutes later the calf lay low in the snow. Hobo feasted, still in peril of his life, for the stags slashed at him as they passed, slashed and trampled on, so obsessed were they with the migration fever.

Next day Hobo drifted on with the caribou herds, ranging on the flank of the procession, watching, waiting; and so he voyaged for many days, for now and then a young caribou would fall lame, and gored and hiked by the rest would drift to the outside edge. There the untrodden snow added to its difficulties, and knowing it was doomed it would at once lose heart.

Down, steadily down now from the tundra heights to the forest again, then one day Hobo stopped, gazing down a long, open defile in the timber. There was nothing to indicate that this was a river, for the snow lay deeply from bank to bank—nothing save the fact that the trees all leant towards the open space, drawn by the light, till their thirst for that element brought them toppling over, their roots undermined at the water's edge.

Here the caribou struck northward; but Hobo stood, still gazing east, gazing down the open aisle

of the forest as though something held him spell-
bound. A passing bull slashed at him, and he
narrowly escaped, then he sat down still gazing
east, glancing back at the drifting host, drifting
away from him towards the north. He uttered a
whine of indecision, for, though he had never
seen this place before, a voice was whispering to
him: " Go east, Hobo, go east!" while another
voice was calling out: " Follow the caribou or
you will starve!"

Hobo rose at length. He trotted to the centre
of the waterway, then eastward he turned, running like the wind, faster now than ever before,
and whining as he ran. " Eastward, Hobo, eastward!" The voice was calling to him, calling him
on like the voices of the children with whom he
had played, or like a mightier voice, harking back
to his puppy days—a voice louder than all other
promptings, echoing down from the buttes and
through the timber slopes, setting at naught all
thoughts of self survival, for now at last the grail
that he had followed was clearly held before his
wondering eyes.

.   .   .   .

When Hobo's master left hospital he was a
broken man, consumed by an all-absorbing thirst
for the northern forests whence he had journeyed
almost a year ago. He wanted to see the aurora
over the tree tops, to hear the wind in the poplars,
to cook his own breakfast over the cabin stove,
to haul up the fish trap through the hole in the
ice after the daily round of his marten sets. He

thought often of his dog who had shared all these things with him, but he dared not try to conjecture what had become of Hobo—him the ugliest dog that ever wagged a yaller tail!

The doctors warned the boy of the folly of returning yet awhile to live alone in that north country, but they knew the futility of arguing thus with a man on whom the solitudes had once cast their spell; so Hobo's master returned—back to the shanty on the Mattagami River, there to spend the remaining winter in one-man loneliness.

But somehow the place seemed changed. The very wind in the poplar ridge sang a sadder song, a song of life's utter emptiness and of the futility of ambition—seemed veritably to mock at his own weakness when he staggered and almost fell during the day's simplest tasks. He did not realize that the change was within himself, that he was a sick man, and that when again the wild geese honked and boomed their way across the sky, the joy of life would come flooding back to him with the dawning of spring, and with all its bright tomorrows.

So, utterly alone, the boy sank deeper and deeper into the sea of despondency, till his weary brain cried for relief, yearned for oblivion; and like many another lonely woodsman, falling foul of sickness, he decided to take the future into his own puny hands in the only way man can do it. And that was just what the doctors had feared.

One evening Hobo's master cleaned the stove, tidied the bench, and placed everything ship-shape and in order.

From his pack the boy took an automatic pistol and thrust a new clip into place. He sat down at the edge of his bunk, thinking of the men and women he had known, wondering what they found in life, wondering why they laughed. Outside the wind howled and the dry snow beat against the shutters. The lamp was going down, and a thin train of smoke rose from the chimney, to vanish like human hosts into thinner air. The same old sounds, the same old scenes! He raised the pistol to his temple, and then—then his hand fell and he sat staring wide-eyed into space.

It was not a sound he had heard. No, there were no sounds outside save those with which he was too familiar. Yet something seemed to have motioned to him, to have clutched his very fingers —not fear either, for he was not afraid, nor was it instinctive nausea at the thing he was about to do. His pulse was steady, he was deadly cool, and deadly prepared, yet he sat there waiting expectantly, straining every sense to hitch on to something tangible, something that assuredly existed in the outer gloom of his consciousness.

It came—a faint shuffling out in the snow, the sound of a heavy breath, of something dragging across the veranda! Then a low whine, a feeble scratching at the door, and again the sound of heavy breathing.

The boy rose. The pistol fell from his grasp and clattered noisily to the floor. He groped his way across the darkening room with hands outstretched, fumbled the latch from its staple, and stood looking down in the snow.

No need to tell what he saw—Hobo stretched out at his feet; Hobo, panting up into his face with hungry, yearning eyes; Hobo, too weary to drag himself another yard, too footsore to stand now that he had fallen; Hobo, the ugliest dog in all the world, staring up into his master's face with joy, such joy and triumph in his bulging bull-dog eyes! He was trying to speak, pouring out his poor, dumb soul in a jumble of weary, guttural noises which to some people might have seemed absurd.

The boy was on his knees now, his arms round the ugliest of ugly dogs, and he too babbled in meaningless nothingnesses, which to the dog meant everything in the world. He carried Hobo to the stove, fed him by hand on the choicest fare the cabin could provide, bathed and bandaged his bleeding foot, and then at length they sat and stared at each other. " You wonderful dog!" cried the boy, and in his voice was something of the world's romance. He rose to his feet and flung out his arms as though to cast something from him, something dark and hideous. " Back to the old life, Hobo!" he cried, " back to the dear old woods again!" Then he fell face foremost on his bunk and sobbed.

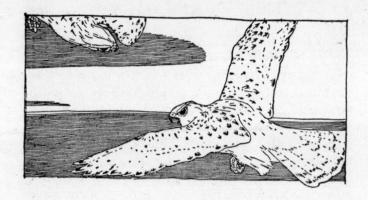

KINGS OF THE INFINITE

I

For nights past Wells, as he lay in his bunk, had listened to the beating of wings high overhead— to the " honk-honk " of countless thousands of wild geese passing northwards to the Arctic, to the plaintive whistling of millions of plovers, dunlins, sand-pipers, knots, and curlews heading for the Alaska sloughs. They came from the sheltered wastes of the Missouri levels, these ghost legions, from the Gulf States, where many had wintered, and were following the eastern slopes of the Rockies by that recognized bird route which leads to the region of half-lights, or farther still to the land of Midnight Sun.

To Wells it was almost maddening. For months past, when he lay sleeping, no sound had broken the upland wastes of the great mountain pass, save once or twice he had started from his dreams as an overloaded cedar, away down the gulch, had cast off its burden of snow, or when a lynx momentarily made the night hideous by an echoing screech of temper. Now the very air was alive, the whole valley throbbing with sound, and Wells, though a young man with a love for the wild, tossed and cursed and buried his head, but eternally found himself listening.

It was always so with the dawning spring; but when at the end of a week the nocturnal procession began to tail off, a reversion set in. He found himself wondering vaguely at the renewed night quietude. All day ruffed grouse drummed in the thickets, blue birds sang everywhere, but night brought silence, stabbed at intervals by the crazy laughter of a loon.

Then came the first thunderstorm. It was evening and Wells sat at the door of his cabin, his eyes upon the heavens. Away down the pass, towards the lovely Kootenays, there hung a jet-black cloud, like a curtain of night across the sky. The edges of it were all torn and jagged, and where the buttes pierced it there was a suggestion of movement—of smoke-like, whirling movement, as though a feathered multitude were wheeling to alight. The air became stifling, but away over the prairies to the east the sunlight still fell in slanting shafts. A golden land it lay, vast and fairy-like, one of those " never-never lands " that belong always to the far distance.

There was a scream overhead, wild, panic-stricken, like the scream of a crazy woman fleeing from the terrors of the coming storm. Wells

looked up and saw—saw the last of the migrants!
The very sky was black with them, darting, criss-
crossing, wheeling in fantastic circles, or plunging
to earth in breathless swoops. From where Wells
sat he could see the white slashes across their
tapered wings, could hear the vibrating purr of
a million beating pinions, and an exclamation
involuntarily broke from his lips, " Gee-e-e, the
thunder birds!"

Thunder birds they assuredly were, hanging to
the very fringe of the bursting cloud, fleeing before
it like a host of racing imps before the spears of
the Thunder King. Two minutes ago not a bird
was to be seen, now they were everywhere, so far
as the eye could see; sweeping towards the open
prairie as heralds of the coming storm. Faster
than the wind they must have travelled—and see!
see! There is one, a speck in the east, he is overhead, he is a mile away, he is lost. They are not
birds at all, but things of the ether, that now and
then take on terrestrial shape to be borne on the
wings of the infinite.

Wells watched and marvelled; then higher
even than the thunder birds, so high above the
towering buttes that they hung as the merest
specks, were two other wheeling atoms of life.
Their gliding flight betrayed them for what they
were, hunters of the upper air, truly of the upper
air, following at the heels of this racing army, as
the wolves once hung to the heels of the buffalo
herds. Not eagles, not vultures, not buzzards, for
none of those would pit their speed against those
aerial acrobats, would choose the swiftest of the

swift to outmanœuvre and outfly in limitless space.
What were they and why—why in the name of
all that's wonderful did they choose to pursue
these winged phantoms when all the woods were
rich in stupid life?

Then, as he watched, Wells saw. A thunder
bird came hurtling earthwards, pinwheeling,
spinning, screaming as it fell, swift as a thunder-
bolt, rejoicing in the headlong plunge, and one
of the wheeling specks above paused in its glide,
then it, too, came on earthwards in pursuit. It
did not swoop, it did not simply fall, but it shot
downwards through space; shot with lashing
wings, straight as a falling stone, but faster, faster
than any stone would fall. The night-hawk
dropped a thousand feet, pinwheeled and fluttered five hundred more, then looped the loop
and shot straight skywards in crazy, zigzag
bounds.

But the falling cannon ball was there to meet
it. A frenzied scream rang through the air, those
white-slashed wings came spinning down once
more, the bird of prey in hot pursuit, till it seemed
to Wells that both would dash themselves to bits
against the spires of the timber line. The man
jumped up, to see the thunder bird recover,
doubling and twisting through the spires, but the
hawk was upon it in a trice. There was a thud,
a cloud of silken feathers, and as the big bird
rose on lazy, gliding wings, its quivering victim
in its talons, Wells saw upon its breast the ermine
of kings—a noble white falcon, swifter even than
the peregrine, and beautiful as it was rare.

" Gee! Gee! You kingly beast!" said Wells aloud, as the falcon wheeled above his head not fifty yards away. " I thought them thunder birds could fly to beat the band, but you—you——" and expression failed him.

Then, as he stared, the hawk let go its noble prize, struck down for the glory of the chase, and the white-slashed phantom came toppling to earth, to fall at the feet of the wondering man; and as he stooped to raise it a thunder spot fell upon his hand, and looking up he saw the sky was empty —the screaming horde had vanished into space.

II

High in a fissure of Last Man Mountain, in a great rugged staircase that ran up the face of the precipice just below that rugged pile where a whole city lies buried, the two gyr-falcons were building their eyrie. They were evidently last year's birds, for their choice of locality was new, and Wells, who thought that as they had come with the thunder birds they would assuredly vanish with the latter, soon learnt his error. The thunder birds he saw no more till the next storm came, when again they swarmed in teeming clouds across the sky, but the very next morning a wild, shrill " kee-kee " in the heavens brought him to his door. Hanging against the sun were the two wheeling falcons, and thereafter he would sit for hours, marvelling at the gliding majesty of their flight. He thought they were migrants from the sunny south like all the rest, for he had no way of knowing that these great white hawks had come from the north, from the lands of eternal snow—had come, with others of their race, to meet the migrating millions.

One evening Wells decided that he wanted fish, so taking his " fish-pole " he wandered down to the creek, and began to flog the water. The fish were rising well, and the squatter, picking his precarious way along a slimy shelf, was suddenly startled by a " whirr " of wings directly overhead. He looked up to see a white flash bearing down upon him, and instinctively he hid his eyes. Not an instant too soon, for now he received a stinging blow straight across the face. There hung the falcon, on quivering wings, not two yards away, preparing to strike again; but the woodsman hit out savagely with his rod and beat it off. He put his hand to his forehead—it was red with blood.

" You brute!" he hissed. " I'll be even with you for that!" And scanning the cliff above he saw the falcon alight high in the fissure. He focused his glasses on the spot and caught the edge of a huge pile of sticks.

" Them young ones will be worth a few dollars when fully fledged," he summed things up, and made a mental resolve to climb the fissure, which looked easily accessible, in a few weeks' time.

In appearance there was little difference between the two falcons, for both were superb and majestic in their ermine robes. The female was a good deal the larger of the two, her wings were less tapered, designed for lifting in addition to speed, but in character they were widely different. For gliding grace of flight she was perhaps the more wonderful to watch, but for dashing, breathless speed, for unexpectedness of attack, the tercel stood alone among all feathered things. It was he who struck the thunder bird from the sky—it was he who struck Wells in the face. His system was to strike first and inquire later, and very often this subsequent inquiry elicited the most surprising facts.

The nest was soon completed—a huge structure of twisted roots and green spruce tips, not neat, not very secure on the edge of its protruding shelf, yet, in its very roughness, clearly the work of blue-blooded birds of prey. It remained only to be lined, and all that day Wells noticed the two falcons skimming back and forth across the valley, swooping high as they gained the timber belt, and speeding up the mountainside till the timber line lay far below, and there towered above only the naked buttes. Here, in a sheltered hollow, they would vanish, and knowing that in that hollow there was a sheep lick, to which the big-horn wild sheep came half across the range to lick the rocks of salt, Wells wondered what attraction this place could have for the falcons. It never occurred to him that where there were sheep there was likely to be wool, and that it was this the hawks were after.

Flying back and forth, each with a contribution, the hen bird would carefully weave the tufts of wool into the twisted fabric, while the male looked on; then off they would go together, buffeting each other as they flew, to glide across the wide valley with its gushing creek, its shadowy uplands touched with the lighter green of birch and poplar. Away to the east lay the endless greyness of the prairies with the transcontinental line, the artery of the waste, threading endlessly on, and away in the distance still, farther than human eye could see, lay Medicine Hat like a field of mushrooms.

Three eggs were laid, and in due course three little thistle-seeds of hunger broke from the shells. Wells knew to the day when this happened, for of late he had many times found game struck down and left almost untouched, the hawks having partaken of the scantiest epicurean meal. Many such trophies found their way to the woodsman's stew-pot, and when one morning he saw the tercel flying heavily, with a whole mountain hare in its talons, he knew that the crowning glory of the spring was theirs at last.

The young birds grew apace, and often now, when the dawn fringed the buttes with liquid gold, Wells heard their screams of eagerness, as one or the other of their parents arrived with food. Quietly the human brute awaited a convenient date for making a trip to the city, and then one morning he took his rope, slipped a light automatic in his belt, and made his way across the creek.

Oh, little falcons, this is a day when your fate hangs in the balance! The skies are your heritage, boundlessly free, the whole wide world is yours, from sea to sea, from range to prairie waste, free

as the wind, free to all the skies, yet a life of
fettered bondage hovers near. You do not understand, you *cannot* understand, or now you would
creep from the eyrie edge and dash yourselves to
death below! Death—death! Is that not less
than bondage for such a thing as you?

But it happened that one other hunter had
heard the screams of the young falcons that golden
dawn, and peering down from a shelf above saw
the three white balls of down in the centre of the
heap of sticks. A red light came into the hunter's
eyes, and bounding lightly from shelf to shelf it
made its sinuous way down the fissure. It was a
devilish beast, low and bear-like in build, skunk-
like in manner of progression, but its face—oh,
its face!—was a mixture between the worst of
the musk-bearing weasel tribe and that perfect
embodiment of sin, the Tasmanian Devil. This
brute was a wolverine; the most perfectly and
terribly equipped instrument of torture Satan has
seen fit to include among his tares.

The tercel, wheeling in mid-heaven a mile
away, saw the wolverine descending, and hurried
to the spot. It was seldom he really hurried; his
pursuit of the thunder bird had been merely a
nose dive. But now, as he saw, he uttered a
piercing " kew ". The sound commenced as he
began to come, and when it was finished he was
almost there. He had often uttered that cry, but
never before had it borne such horror and alarm.
It sent his wife rocketing giddily sky-wards from
nowhere in particular; then she too saw, and
together they met the foe.

They met him on a narrow shelf, deep with drift sand from above, and as they came the wolverine backed against the rocks with a screech of warning. Dauntlessly the hawks came on, lashed him with their wings, and rebounded quick as light as those terrible claws slashed out at them.

The wolverine was sitting now, grizzly fashion, his jaws apart, his small pig-eyes blood red. The tercel flashed to the shelf, his wings winnowing at invisible speed. The wolverine dashed at him, not in self defence but eager for food, then writhed back with a hiss of dismay as a whirling sand-blast met his eyes. The female alighted the other side, and she too beat the air, beat up a cyclone of sand, blinding, stinging, a blast not even a weasel could have faced.

The wolverine was taken unawares. Beaks and claws he did not fear, he would even turn and fight fire, but fighting a sand-storm was beyond his scope. He was blinded, stifled, lost as to which way to turn. With a screech he leapt for the perpendicular rock, and as he fell back, clawing, hissing, a dozen razor blades slashed across his face, laid open his scalp from eye to eye. And all the time the sand-blast was going on.

Could he face it? Could he find a way of retreat? No! A wolverine is never beaten, and blinded now with his own life blood, dripping saliva and hatred from his jaws, he charged into the cyclone with lowered head.

The falcons rose, as though drawn by a wire from above, and again those razor blades slashed the fiendish one across the eyes. He buried his face between his paws and rolled with ready claws, but there was no one—*nothing* there!

Over the edge and down he went, striking the shelves, ricochetting, screaming, till there was no scream left in him; and the falcons descended too, striking as he fell, and uttering aloft their shrill " kee-kees " of triumph.

Wells, in the act of mounting the fissure far below, knew nothing of all this till he heard the falcons descending upon him, then he threw his back to the rocks, the small automatic in one hand, a stone in the other. Something struck the rock above his head, rebounded, fell with a thud at his feet, and lay there quivering. It was the dead wolverine.

The falcons saw and wheeled away, and the young man looked at the hideous thing at his feet, saw the open gashes across its face, from eye to eye and from nose to crown, and shuddered as he thought of that awful vengeance. How narrowly he himself had escaped it, and this quivering mass of carrion, a few seconds ago the fiercest fighter in all the wild, dashed from the shelf in the moment of triumphant robbery, was to Wells as a warning from above to follow his pursuit no further. He climbed slowly down. " Well, I'll be blessed!" he muttered. " A wolverine of all beasts! Them falcons ain't for me, but a good wolverine pelt was worth coming for."

.   .   .   .

The wolves are not yet gone from the prairie

foothills, and the squatter one evening saw a solitary wolf cross the plateau below his claim. Wolf bounties were high, even though skins were poor, and close by the old buffalo trail, by the margin of the creek, Wells set a No. 4 wolf trap.

That evening the tercel came gliding down the creek, looking for musquash or squirrels, when, close by the old trail, amidst the graceful golden rod, something white moved as the wind veered. It was only the wing of a white hen, lashed to the spring plate of the settler's trap, so as to rouse the curiosity of any passing wolf, but, as usual, the falcon struck without a second look, prepared to inquire into the matter later. His talons met the bone-dry earth with a thud, and out of the sand there rose a terrible monster. It caught the falcon high up on the legs, the blunt jaws closing with a vice-like grip, and he fell with a scream of terror, his wonderful wings outspread. For an hour he fought and tussled, filling the air with sand and feathers, then at length he lay very still like a limp white cloth across the trail.

Out of the purple haze his mate called to him, wondering why he did not bring food to their little ones, and her voice rang in a thin-edged blade of sound across the vastness of the evening calm. He answered with a plaintive " kew ", as though half to himself, but she heard it. Here she came, high in the heavens, a gliding floating speck against a sunset of rose and gold, glorious in her boundless freedom. She hung in mid-air among the gossamer clouds, and again that faint, thin voice, almost too fine and far for human ears to catch, floated down to him, and again he answered. She stood still now, suspended in the sky, and looked down at the poor trampled thing there in the dust. It could not be her lord, oh no! She circled off to search for him elsewhere, and he watched her go.

The sun died behind the buttes, that city of purple castles in endless array, melting into the distance till rugged turret and gold-rimmed cloud became one dream of vastness. The grouse ceased their drumming, moths hummed in the fragrant air, and all along the great blue range the lakes lay like burnished silver.

A lone, lank wolf came down the trail and looked at the white bird from afar. His eyes shone, he licked his chops, and had the falcon so much as stirred, he would have bounded in with a chop of jaws. But the bird lay very still, and the wolf began to dally round in ever-narrowing circles. On the windward side the scent of steel smote his nostrils. His mane bristled, he uttered a rumbling growl, and began to scratch with all four legs. Then, still rumbling over his shoulder, he trotted off, and the falcon was spared.

Day came with its torturing heat and thirst, and the kingly creature of the clouds struggled again to rise aloft. Wells, at his cabin door, saw those beating wings, and smiled grimly to himself.

An hour or so later the man went down to the plateau, a club in his hand. The falcon reared to meet him, helpless but defiant, and they looked into each other's eyes.

" Now I've got you, you little varmint,"

muttered the man. " Now I'll pay you out for hitting me in the face."

Yet, even as he spoke, he knew that the club in his hand was a mockery of himself. He felt his manhood quiver, or was it his manhood that rose in passionate revolt? There are some things we cannot destroy, and as Wells looked into those eyes he stood on the border of that land where such things live. Wonderful eyes they were, of flashing crystal, purer than gold, clearer than amber, and in the centre of each was a tiny point of fire. The broad white chest, barred with deeper shades, caught the slanting sunbeams and reflected silver. Was ever a king more glorious, more grand, more fearlessly noble in the hour of utter defeat?

The club fell from the man's limp fingers, he was on his knees in the sand. The loneliness, the long, long silence, had perhaps made him a little mad, yet in his madness there was a wisdom that most men lose with the going of their childhood days. " Oh, you wonderful, wonderful thing," he thought. " How I should have rejoiced to see you in my twelfth year or thereabouts, when all the world was new; and now, because of your glory, I cannot harm you. Go, little aeronaut, go to the skies and flash in the sunlight above the clouds. It is there you belong—to immeasurable space. Go, little pirate, and if ever we meet again remember this—that once in my hands there lay for the taking the most priceless thing God ever gave to bird—your life.

" Farewell. I cannot steal from God."